D1635074

DUNGEON

OF

DOOM

Another 'You Say Which Way' Adventure
by
Peter Friend

Published by:
The Fairytale Factory Ltd.
Wellington, New Zealand.
All rights reserved.
Copyright Peter Friend © 2017

No part of this book may be copied,
stored, or transmitted in any form
or by any means, without prior
permission of the author.

ISBN-13: 978-1544879451

ISBN-10: 1544879458

How This Book Works

- This story depends on YOU.

- YOU say which way the story goes.

- What will YOU do?

At the end of each chapter, you get to make a decision. Turn to the page that matches your choice – for example, **P62** means turn to page 62.

You've unlocked a secret bonus level while playing *Dungeon of Doom* with your friends, and were magically transported inside the game. Now you must work together to finish the level and return to the real world. There are lots of ways to succeed, but even more ways to die. After all, this is *Dungeon of Doom*, not *Ultra-Peaceful Happy Underground Walk of Absolutely No Danger.*

Oh … and watch out for the stone shark, the big rolling head, the hortimancer, and the reverse dragon!

DUNGEON
OF
DOOM

Secret Bonus Level

On Saturday morning, you're sitting around the kitchen table with Jim and Tina, playing *Dungeon of Doom* together on your laptops.

"Gotcha." Jim taps his keyboard to launch another fireball at the Nine-Headed Dragon's eleventh head. (One head grew back. Twice.)

"Yee ha!" Tina's onscreen avatar, Tina Warrior Princess, finally chops off the dragon's last head.

Level Completed appears in giant sparkly letters. The floor of the dungeon room fills with gold coins, gems, roast chickens, healing potions, and other end-of-level bonuses. Your avatar, Velzon the Elven Archer, runs around the room collecting them. Tina Warrior Princess and Jim's avatar, Wizard Zim, do the same.

"Warriors don't say 'yee ha'," Jim complains.

Tina grins. "I'm a *cowgirl* warrior princess, and I'll say 'yee ha' if I want to."

While they're arguing, you spot a weird shimmering circle on the wall by the Nine-Headed Dragon's tail, and walk over to it. "Um, guys," you say.

They're not listening.

"Try to take the game seriously, Tina," Jim says. "There's no such thing as cowgirl warrior princesses."

"Great advice, from a wizard wearing sunglasses," she sneers.

"They're not sunglasses, they're Enchanted Shadow Crystal Lenses. They give a plus 10 bonus when detecting and deciphering magic."

"Yeah, right, and they just happen to look exactly like sung—"

"Hey, Tina Warrior Princess and Wizard Zim!" you interrupt. "What's this mysterious round thingy on the wall in front of me?"

"Huh? What are you jabbering about?" Tina walks around, frowns at your laptop screen, then checks her own again. "My screen just shows ordinary wall there. Weird."

"Mine too," Jim says. "Can't be a magical artefact, coz I can't see it through my Enchanted Shadow Crystal Lenses. So it must be something Elvish."

"Well, duh." Tina rolls her eyes and returns to her chair.

They both look at you expectantly.

Huh! Just because Velzon is a 400-year-old elf, that doesn't make you an expert on mysterious shimmering walls.

You have an idea. Onscreen, you pick up a gold coin and toss it at the shimmery wall. As you'd half-expected, the coin vanishes. At the same moment, the edge of the circle flashes like a camera, and…were those letters?

"The wall flashed on my screen," Tina says. "What is it, a booby trap?"

She could be right.

"It was on my screen too. Might be just a program bug," Jim grumbles. "Remember that level in *Monkey Maniacs*, where jumping on the giant banana made the whole game crash?"

He could be right too.

"I think it's a portal." You toss another coin at it, watching the circle carefully. The letters reappear, and this time you can read them. "It says 'Secret Bonus Level' in Klodruchian runes."

"Cool," Tina whispers. "Whatever a Klod-whatsit is."

Jim sniffs. "I haven't seen anything on the internet about a secret bonus level in *Dungeon of Doom*."

"That makes it even cooler," Tina says. "Maybe we're the first players to find it. We'll be famous. Especially me."

"Why you?" you ask suspiciously.

"Coz I'll be first." Onscreen, Tina Warrior Princess leaps into the shimmering portal.

But you and Jim had the same idea too, and Velzon and Zim leap into the portal at the same time. Everything turns really bright, then really dark, then…

Huh? The whole kitchen's gone, and you're lying on a stone floor. Next to you are a tall woman covered in muscles and scars and battered armor, and a bearded guy in a purple robe and a pointy hat – Tina Warrior Princess and Wizard Zim, looking just like they do in the game, but…now they're real.

Impossible. Totally impossible.

"What happened?" Wizard Zim asks.

You look down. You're wearing Velzon's leaf-embroidered jerkin, spider silk trousers, and lizard-leather boots. Just to be sure, you reach up, and…yup, elf ears. On your back is a bow and quiver. On your belt is a long dagger of finest Kargalin steel. Exactly like in the game.

"We're inside *Dungeon of Doom*." Tina Warrior Princess stands up, a huge grin on her scarred face. "Cool!"

Zim tugs at his beard. "Don't be stupid. We can't be. What is this, some new virtual reality thing?" He turns to you. "I don't like it. Make it stop. Turn it off. Now!"

"How?" you ask.

He runs around the room, yelling, "Reset! End game! Escape! Power off! End simulation! Exit!" Nothing happens.

"Try to take the game seriously, Zim," Tina says with a smirk.

"I have to be home soon for lunch, or Mom will be angry."

"I don't think the great wizard Zim's mommy makes him lunch," you say, trying to make him laugh, but it doesn't work.

"Let's explore!" Tina shouts, and runs out the room's only doorway.

"We might as well. We can't just stay here," you tell Zim.

He crouches beside a pillar. "Why not? This room is nice and quiet, and there are plenty of roast chicken bonuses if I miss lunch."

"That's not how the game works, remember? If we stay in one place for too long, monsters attack us, more and more, until it's wall-to-wall fangs and claws. So we have to explore, to find this level's exit, and... get back to the real world." Well, you hope so.

"Mmm," he says reluctantly, and follows you out the doorway.

Tina's only a few steps away, frowning as she looks up and down a corridor. "This better not be a maze. I hate mazes. Always get lost." She says it like she's joking, but it's the truth – she has a terrible sense of direction, in real life and in games.

Left and right look the same – generic stone-walled dungeon corridors, lit by burning torches, with more doorways in the distance. This level's exit could be either way. Or both ways – some levels have more than one exit.

Zim peers both ways through his Enchanted Shadow Crystal Lenses, then shrugs and looks at you. "Well, pointy ears?"

After listening and sniffing in both directions, you point left. "Goblins. Lots of them." You point right. "Ogres. Coming this way."

Tina and Zim look at you expectantly.

"What, you want *me* to decide?"

Tina grins. "Yeah, Velzon, you're good at that elfy scouting stuff. That's the only reason we let you play with us."

Zim nods. "Let's play this level the same way we usually do – you leading the way."

"So I get shot first, and stabbed first, and zapped first?" you ask.

"No worries, we'll be right behind, ready to rescue you," Tina says.

6

"And I've got a zillion healing potions if you get injured," Zim says.

"Thanks, you two are so helpful."

It's time to make a decision. Do you:

Go left, towards the goblins? **P7**

Or

Go right, towards the ogres? **P63**

The Goblins

You turn left, because goblins are the least scary creatures in a dungeon.

But the goblin smell (like a mixture of wet dog and broccoli) gets stronger with every step you take. Maybe there are hundreds of goblins down this way. Or thousands. A thousand goblins together can kill just about anything, even a giant or a dragon. They'd easily wipe out an elf, a warrior princess, and a wizard. Maybe this direction wasn't such a good idea after all.

You hear the usual goblin sounds too – bickering and growling and grumbling that never stops, even in battle.

At the end of the corridor is an archway flanked by two big statues of frowning demons, one of them fallen. You crouch behind the fallen stone demon and peer through the archway.

Goblins. Hundreds of them, which explains the smell and noise.

What's surprising is that they're clambering up and down a tall rickety platform, and painting a huge mural that covers the entire far wall. Since when have goblins been artistic?

What's even more surprising is that the half-finished mural shows an elf, a warrior princess, and a wizard, who look a lot like the three of you.

"Is this a goblin joke, and they're about to turn and point at us and laugh, before attacking?" whispers Zim.

"Nah, a goblin isn't smart enough to think of that. Their

idea of comedy is giggling while they bite off someone's fingers and toes," Tina whispers.

"I think it must be a magic mural that looks different to anyone who sees it," you whisper. "The goblins don't seem to know they're painting us – or at least, they're paying no attention to this doorway."

Zim nods. "Yeah, don't get close to the mural. That whole wall's crawling with magic. I'm pretty sure the goblins are under a spell. But look over there." He points past the mural and the goblins to a doorway framed by ivy.

"So what?" Tina asks.

"Ivy doesn't grow underground. I think there's daylight through there. It could be this level's exit."

"Or just an outdoorsy part of it," you say. "Remember the outdoorsy part of Level 49, where we were attacked by wolves and struck by lightning and nearly eaten by a tree? Sometimes it's safer to stay indoors. Besides, we've got no way to sneak past the goblins."

"Actually, we do. I found a cool Invisibility spell in my Big Book of Spells, and I've been dying to try it out."

Tina snorts. "Yeah, 'dying' – as in, we usually die whenever you try a new spell."

Die? Oh. "Hey, that's a really good point. What happens if we die?" you ask.

"Huh?"

"If we die here inside the game, what happens? Are we just sent back to our last Save Point? Or," you shiver, "do we die in the real world too?"

Zim whimpers.

Tina looks serious for once. "Yeah, but, um…" She grips her sword and looks around again. "How about that doorway there instead?"

You take a closer look at the shadow she's pointing to. She's right. Within the shadow is a narrow doorway. And it's close. You could probably sneak through it without the goblins noticing, even without an Invisibility spell.

"Yeah, that way is okay too, I guess, but it's not as…ivy-ish as the other way," Zim says, sounding embarrassed. Obviously, he hadn't noticed the narrow doorway either. "But someone's scratched 'Beware' on the wall next to it."

"Beware of what?" you ask. "Beware of the dog? Beware of wet paint? Not very helpful."

"'Beware' is always good advice in a dungeon," Tina says.

It's time to make a decision. Do you:

Turn invisible and sneak past the goblins to the ivy doorway? **P10**

Or

Go through the narrow doorway? **P32**

Invisibly Sneak Past the Goblins

"Okay, Zim, let's try your Invisibility spell and see what's through that doorway with the ivy," you say.

Zim hums, makes a gargling noise, shakes his fingers, and spins his wand from hand to hand.

"Didn't work. We're still totally visible," Tina says.

"I haven't cast the spell yet. That was just my stretching exercises."

She rolls her eyes.

Zim pulls a leather-bound book from his robes and opens it. He mutters, wriggles his fingers, and twirls his wand, faster and faster.

Just as Tina opens her mouth, probably to make another sarcastic comment, she vanishes. So do Zim and you.

"Wow, it actually worked," comes Tina's voice from the empty air. "I take back all the mean things I was going to say about you, Wizard Zim."

"Thanks a lot, Princess Mean-er."

"Let's go. Quietly," you say, before they can start arguing again.

Within seconds, you discover the downside of being invisible – you can't see where you're walking, and can't see each other.

Tina stubs her toe on your boot heel and swears under her breath.

A few seconds later, Zim drops his wand. It clatters on the stone floor and is visible for a moment before he snatches it back up. Luckily, you all stay invisible, and the goblins don't seem to notice.

Or did they? Some of them lower their paint pots and brushes, look around as if puzzled, and sniff with their long pointy noses.

"Smelly!" squeals one. "Bad smelly! Peoples!"

What? They think *you're* smelly? It's surprising they can smell anything except themselves.

The goblins look around everywhere but can't see you.

"Magics!" squeals another goblin.

They glance towards the ivy doorway, whine and whimper to each other, then start painting faster than before. Who or what are they scared of?

Tina collides with you again. She grabs your shoulder, then nudges you forwards. Good idea. Maybe Zim is holding onto her too. Or maybe not. As quietly as possible, you shuffle forwards.

By the time you're halfway past the mural, the goblins are sniffing suspiciously again.

One goblin flings its paint pot and splatters blue paint over the floor, missing you only by a few feet. Other goblins get the same idea, and soon there's paint flying in every direction. They haven't hit you yet, but it's only a matter of time before…

"Wooooh!" A goblin points at the floor.

Oops. You've stepped in wet paint and are leaving a trail of multi-colored footprints.

"Run!" you yell.

The three of you race for the ivy doorway. Well, you do – hopefully Tina and Zim are following.

Dozens of goblins scamper down from the platform and give chase. Luckily, you have a head start, and have longer legs than goblins, and they still can't see more than your footprints.

They're right behind you, but the moment you reach the ivy doorway, they screech to a halt. There's lots of whispering and pointing and shoving, but not one of them is brave enough to step through the doorway, or to touch the ivy.

Good. Although now you're more and more worried about what's in here.

"Master, he sort them out," one says at last.

The others agree and repeat this to each other, nodding and giggling. Then they run back to the mural, leaving hundreds more painty footprints.

"Weird," whispers Tina's voice beside you.

"Totally weird," whispers Zim's voice. "So, we may as well explore and see if this is the exit, right?"

Something rustles in the ivy. You look around. No people or animals are in sight. The walls and floor are covered in thick ivy. It blocks the corridor a bit further along, although maybe you could push or cut a path through. The high ceiling looks like glass blocks, with sunlight shining through them. An indoor garden? Nice, but…in a dungeon?

"Yeah, we might as well look for the exit," Tina says. "I'm not going back out there while those goblins are around.

Nasty little creatures. One of them tried to bite my foot. While giggling."

"But why didn't the goblins follow us in here?" you ask. "They must be terrified of this 'Master', whoever he is. Zim, can you make us visible again? Being invisible isn't nearly as much fun as I expected."

There's no reply.

Tina sighs. "Please, o mighty Wizard Zim, we humbly beg thee to remove thy super cool spell, yeah, thanks."

Still no reply.

"Not funny, Zim, just—"

Just what? Why'd Tina stop talking mid-sentence?

Something rustles in the ivy. Maybe the same something that rustled before. Maybe not.

"Tina? Zim?" You draw your dagger. "Hello? Anyone?"

More silence. You hope this is some stupid joke they're playing, because if not, it's something far worse.

Ivy wraps around your legs, and pulls you towards the deep green shadows. Perhaps it's trying to help you. Or kill you.

It's time to make a decision – and fast, while your arms are still free. Do you:

Cut yourself free with your dagger? **P14**

Or

Follow the ivy? **P16**

Chop the Ivy

You slash at the ivy with your dagger.

The green tendrils part and fall away, but more replace them.

You slash again, but your dagger's not much of a pruning knife. Soon, ivy wraps your hands and feet, squeezing in a deadly embrace. It sprouts into your nose, your ears, your eyes, until…

Suddenly you're back in the real world, alone, scrunched up on the kitchen floor and gasping for breath.

On the table above you, the words *Game Over* sparkle on your laptop screen.

Huh? Why are you on the floor? Weren't you playing with your friends? Where are they, and…why can't you even remember their names?

On the far side of the room, a pot plant's leaves quiver in a draft. For some reason that you can't explain, you shiver.

Sorry, this part of your story is over – you were squeezed to death by angry ivy.

If you'd made different choices, things might have gone better (or even worse).

Have you met the Emerald Sage? Gotten lost in the maze? Been attacked by the bone army? Run from the giant rolling head? Helped the extremely wet queen? Said hello to the Reverse Dragon? Avoided the Zenobian Snapper?

It's time to make a decision. Do you:

Go back to the previous section? **P10**

Or

Go back to the beginning of the story and try another path? **P113**

Or

Go to the great big list of choices? **P118**

Follow the Ivy

A forest of ivy pushes and pulls you through its tangled vines. Your bow and quiver are ripped from your back, but you desperately hold on to the dagger with both hands, determined not to be left defenseless.

Eventually the ivy dumps you into an empty room. Instead of hitting the hard stone floor, you land on something soft and invisible.

"Ow," says Zim's voice.

"Wasn't me," says Tina's voice.

"It's me, Velzon," you say. "Zim, invisibility's really annoying – can you cancel the spell?"

"No, I lost my wand in the ivy. Along with my healing potions, my wizard's hat, and my left boot. I even lost my Big Book of Spells."

"Big Book of Spells?" sneers a deep voice.

You turn. A tall green figure stands in a dark doorway.

"No proper wizard needs to carry a book of spells. Show yourselves, worms!" He waves a wand. Actually, it looks more like a twig, but it must be a wand, because you, Tina and Zim are suddenly visible again. Zim looks miserable, and Tina's lost her weapons in the ivy too.

You try to hide your dagger behind your back, but…it's been magically transformed into a daffodil.

The tall figure moves out of the doorway, revealing he's actually a short figure wearing a very tall green hat, so tall that the tip scrapes along the glass ceiling. His robes and boots are also green. Even his long white beard's a bit greenish – moss or mold, perhaps.

Scowling, he looks you all up and down, then turns to Zim. "Pathetic. More pathetic than my goblin watchdogs out there. A third-rate wizard like you thought you could march in here with your bodyguards and steal her from me?"

"Third-rate?" Zim sounds insulted.

"You think we're Zim's bodyguards?" Tina sounds even more insulted.

"Steal who?" you ask. "We don't want to steal anyone from anyone. We're just looking for the exit, sir."

"Oh really? What a coincidence – my last so-called visitors said the same thing. And claimed they'd never heard of me, the world-famous Emerald Sage. Hah!" He gestures with his wand at an ivy-covered wall, and the vines obediently shrink back, revealing a corridor. "Move."

You've never heard of a wizard called the Emerald Sage, but you aren't going to tell him that. As an elf, you've seen enough plant magic to realize this guy must be a powerful hortimancer, and you don't want to be turned into a daffodil.

Tina gets to her feet, clenching a fist while twitching her nose, which is her secret signal for *How about I punch this guy's face off?*

You shake your head – you don't want her turned into a daffodil either.

Zim stands uncomfortably in one boot and one bare foot.

"Um, could I please have my other boot back, Mr. Sage, sir?"

The Emerald Sage waves his twig wand, and suddenly Zim's bare foot is a boot-sized block of solid wood. "Any more complaints?" he sneers.

"No, sir," you all chorus, and march down the corridor in front of him, Zim going step-thud-step-thud-step-thud with his wooden foot.

"What sort of name's Emerald Sage?" Tina mutters. "Sounds like an ingredient in my dad's spaghetti sauce recipe."

"Shush," you whisper.

The ivy ends, replaced by what look like Venus fly-traps, except these have eyes and turn to stare at you.

"Keep your distance," the Emerald Sage warns. "They're hungry."

Another part of his security system, apparently. He sure is paranoid.

The next corridor has daffodils growing everywhere. You tip-toe through them, trying not to step on any, just in case they're magically transformed previous adventurers.

The corridor leads to an untidy workroom, lined with shelves of pot plants and cobwebbed leather-bound books. Above a mantelpiece is a painting of busy goblins with paintbrushes. The picture's moving! Oh, that's the room you were in before. The painting must be some sort of magical security video monitor. Several long tables and the floor are stacked with more books, crumpled pages of parchment, quill pens, bottles of ink, and three rusty watering cans.

The far wall has an archway with words carved into it. Beyond is a large room, full of tangled thorn bushes, except for a stone platform with a bed on it.

In the bed, someone's snoring.

"Sleeping Beauty," you, Zim and Tina say at the same time. This isn't the first weird fairytale you've encountered in *Dungeon of Doom*. There were three grumpy porridge-loving bears on Level 82.

"Yes," the Emerald Sage says dreamily. "Princess Valeria is the most beautiful woman in the world."

Um, that's not what you meant, but never mind. As far as you can see through the thorns, the sleeping princess is in her seventies. About the same age as the Emerald Sage. Oh.

"Is she your one true love, sir?" you ask.

"Not yet," the Emerald Sage says. "But when I release her from the spell, she'll be so grateful that she'll fall in love with me."

Is he really that dumb?

Tina rolls her eyes. She hates kissy stuff.

"And for how long have you been trying to free Princess Valeria, sir?" you ask, still in your politest voice.

"Fifty-two years."

Wow. Zim gasps, and Tina lets out a strangled giggle. You glare at them.

The Emerald Sage raises his wand, as if he's about to turn you all into daffodils or worse. "Back when my beloved Valeria was enchanted, I was just a young apprentice royal wizard, and I couldn't do anything against such a powerful spell. But I've been studying ancient tomes and arcane lore ever since, and now I'm very close to breaking it."

Uh-oh. You're not sure what arcane lore is, but he's definitely doing a Super-Villain speech and explaining his evil plans, which probably means you're about to die horribly.

Sure enough, he gives a creepy smile. "Now I need some volunteers to walk into the thorns when I cast my counter-spell."

You peer through the thorns again. Dozens of skeletons are intertwined in the branches, and more litter the floor. Probably previous "volunteers".

Tina and Zim sidle up to you.

"Let's make a run for it," Tina whispers. "I don't trust his stupid counter-spell."

"No, this must be a logic puzzle, like on Level 59," whispers Zim. "If we can help him solve it, that will break the spell, and the Sage will give us a huge reward. Besides, the level exit's probably behind those thorns."

It's time to make a decision. Do you:

Make a run for it? **P21**

Or

Try to break the spell? **P23**

Run for It

The Emerald Sage turns towards the princess for a moment. You nod to Tina and Zim, and the three of you run for the doorway. Not as quietly as you'd hoped – Zim's wooden foot thumps on the floor with every second step.

Something behind you zaps, and…

Suddenly you're back in the real world.

But something's wrong. Very wrong. There's the kitchen, and the table, and three laptops, looking perfectly normal. Except…you're in a bath? With two giant yellow flowers next to you? Oh, you're a giant yellow flower too. No, this isn't a bath, it's an ordinary vase on the window sill, which means…

"He turned us into daffodils," you tell the other two flowers – presumably Jim and Tina.

Or at least, you try to speak, except you don't have a mouth. Whoever heard of talking flowers? That makes you want to laugh, except you can't laugh either. Then you can't remember what was funny, and then you can't remember anything at all. Everything turns a beautiful shade of emerald green. Forever.

Sorry, this part of your story is over. If you'd made different choices, things might have gone better (or even worse). Have you gotten lost in the maze? Been attacked by the bone army? Run from the giant rolling head? Helped the extremely wet queen? Said hello to the Reverse Dragon?

Avoided the Zenobian Snapper?

It's time to make a decision. Do you:

Go back to the previous section? **P16**

Or

Go back to the beginning of the story and try another path? **P113**

Or

Go to the great big list of choices? **P118**

Break the Spell

"Okay, Zim, let's try to break the spell," you whisper, hoping he knows what he's doing.

He turns to the Emerald Sage. "I'm nowhere near as great a wizard as you are, sir, but I might be able to help. What type of spell it is? Hyper-dimensional Glass? Daemonic Vortex Wall?"

Is he making this stuff up?

"Curse of Eternal Thorns," the Emerald Sage snaps. "Isn't that obvious? Why else would I spend fifty-two years studying hortimancy?"

Okay, apparently all wizards really do talk like this. What a pair of nerds.

Zim nods. "Of course, I should have thought of Curse of Eternal Thorns. That explains the, um, thorns. What's the spell's thaumaturgical constriction?"

The Emerald Sage snorts and points to the words carved around the stone archway. "A cryptic prophecy. Such a cliché."

The words read:

> *Below the earth, in caverns deep,*
> *the princess shall forever sleep,*
> *bewitched, until a worthy mind*
> *can slay the thorns, not thorns, and find*
> *beneath these words, the truth. Or else*

The last stone is blank.

"Or else what? Why's the final line missing?" Zim picks

up a long parchment page from a table. It's the words from the archway, copied out a dozen times, with words underlined or circled or crossed out or translated into other languages. The whole page is marked with arrows and scribbly diagrams and notes in terrible tiny handwriting. "Hmm. What does the prophecy mean, sir?"

"Nothing," the Emerald Sage snarls. "I wasted years trying to decipher it, but it's just a red herring, a distraction. Forget it. I've spent the last few years researching a rare counter-spell called Botanical Discombobulation. I'm fairly sure I've got it right this time."

Only "fairly sure"? That's not reassuring.

"Zim's great at deciphering prophecies," you say, hoping to gain some more time.

"Um, yeah." Zim looks uncertainly at the parchment and back to the archway.

"Yeah, totally," Tina adds. "He's an ace at prophecies, crosswords, and Sudoku."

The Emerald Sage furrows his brow. "Cross Words? Sudoku? I've never heard of such spells. Perhaps you are wiser than you seem, Zim. Or perhaps you're trying to trick me, just like all those others over the years. Let's find out."

He waves his wand, and all three of you take a step towards the archway. Then another step.

"What's happening?" Tina asks. "My feet are moving by themselves."

"He's cast Inexorable March on us," Zim moans. "We'll keep walking, no matter what."

She tries punching her legs, but that doesn't stop her taking another step. "We're headed for those sharp thorns."

The Emerald Sage giggles. "This is your chance to demonstrate the power of Sudoku. Or die. Good luck, I want you to succeed, I really do. I'll be right here, casting Botanical Discombobulation." He waves his wand again and begins chanting. Beyond the gateway, the thorny branches start to bend out of the way, creating a path towards old Sleeping Beauty. Great, except that the bent branches are quivering, as if only held there by invisible hands, ready to spring back at you at any moment.

"Any ideas about the prophecy, guys?" You try to hold onto a table, but the spell's too strong.

Tina shrugs. "Don't ask me, I hate poetry."

"Think of the lines as song lyrics," Zim tells her. "Prophecies always mean something important. There must be a clue in there somewhere."

"Below the earth, in caverns deep," she warbles, off-key, while playing air guitar. "Yeah, I can imagine my favorite death metal band thrashing out a song like that. But what does 'thorns, not thorns' mean anyway? And who goes around slaying thorns? Doesn't make sense."

Behind you, the Emerald Sage continues chanting. Another step. You're at the archway.

"That's the whole point, it's a paradox," you say, then realize what you just said. "Um, yeah, perhaps the thorns aren't really thorns."

"They're not cuddly teddy bears!" Zim snaps.

You try but fail to hold on to the archway. Your next step gives you an uncomfortably close look at the quivering thorns. If the Emerald Sage's Botanical Discombobulation spell fails now, you'll be skewered.

Hmm, why are the thorns in pairs, like…tiny fangs? Ah. "Zim, do you have any spells that slay snakes?"

His eyes widen. "Probably, in my Big Book of Spells, but I don't have that or my wand anymore."

"Anything that could work on a room full of snakes? Anything at all? Think fast!"

"Well, there's Serpentine Snooze, I suppose. Every junior wizard learns to cast that. It doesn't even need a wand. But no, that's far too easy."

You take another involuntary step, and a pair of thorns (or maybe fangs) presses into your arm. Ouch, they really hurt. And what if they're poisonous? "Try it, Zim, now!"

He waves his arms like the world's worst disco dancer, while chanting something that sounds like a drain unblocking. The thorny branches shudder and drop to the floor, falling apart into, yes, snakes. Great, now you're surrounded by a roomful of hissing snakes. But before you can make an Indiana Jones joke, they slither into the room's corners and…fall asleep. Maybe from Zim's spell, or perhaps they're exhausted from pretending to be thorns for fifty-two years.

"What have you done?" the Emerald Sage squeals. "Don't you dare kiss her, she's mine." He dashes past, heading for the bed on the platform.

"Ew, I wasn't going to kiss anyone," Tina mutters.

Zim giggles.

Before the Emerald Sage reaches the old woman, she wakes and sits up.

"Took you long enough, Norman," she says. "Partly my own fault, I admit. I had such fun writing that prophecy, even though I couldn't think of a good rhyme for 'Or Else', so I never finished it. And then I had to cast the spell in a mad rush, and it was my first spell ever, and I think I mispronounced a few words."

"You cast the spell on yourself?" squeaks the Emerald Sage (apparently also known as Norman). "But why? How? You're a princess, not a wizard."

"Being a princess was so boring. Mom and Dad were trying to marry me off to every second prince who walked past, and I hadn't met even one I liked. Such a bunch of fools." She pulls a thick book from under her pillow. "One day, I found this old book in the library, full of exciting spells. I thought, why not create a magical puzzle and see which prince is smart enough to solve it? I expected someone would work it out in a few days or weeks at most. But none of them did. Everyone gave up after a month or so. Except you, not-prince Norman."

He blushes.

"But, still, fifty-two years?" she continues. "And then these three solve it for you?" She points at you, Zim and Tina, still slowly marching towards her platform.

Norman's mouth opens and closes as if he's a goldfish.

"Just a lucky guess," you say, feeling sorry for him.

Tina and Zim nod.

"Well, at least you never gave up on me, Norman," she says kindly. "I appreciate that. I'm terribly thirsty. Let's have a chat over a nice cup of tea. People still drink tea, don't they? Good. Come on, dear." She takes his hand, walks over to a doorway in the far wall, and leads him up a flight of stairs.

Leaving you here?

"Excuse me!" you shout. "Emerald Sage? Sir? Could you cancel your Inexcusable March spell, please?"

There's no reply.

"Inexorable March," Zim corrects.

Tina turns to the doorway and yells, "Hey, Emerald Parsley, cut this marching stuff and give us our huge reward for breaking the snakey spell for you!"

Silence. They've gone.

"Ungrateful sod!" she yells.

All of you take another step and stub your toes on the platform for the hundredth time. Splinters fall off Zim's wooden foot.

"Princess Sleepy Head was no better, just walked off and left us," Tina continues. "Princesses are awful, can't be trusted."

"But you're a princess," Zim points out.

"No, no, us warrior princesses are okay. Obviously. It's those non-warrior princesses you have to watch out for."

Another step. Ow. Why are Zim and Tina wasting time

yacking about princesses?

"Can't you do something to break this marching spell?" you ask Zim.

He shakes his head. "Not without my Big Book of Spells."

"How about that one?" Tina points to the book left by the old princess.

"Oh, yeah, didn't think of that." He stretches out, manages to grab the book by its corner, and flicks through the pages. "Hey, this is a cool book, much better than my old one."

"Hurry, my toes are getting sorer and sorer. I'm sure I've broken a toenail."

Your toes hurt too.

"Okay, okay, I found a Mystical Dispellation spell that should work," Zim says, "but I don't have a wand. Even a twig or a pencil would do."

You point to the splinters by his wooden foot. "What about one of those?"

He picks up a thin sliver of wood and frowns. "A bit small. But here goes." He waves the "wand" and recites something that sounds like a goat arguing with a dolphin. Suddenly you can move your own feet again. What a relief.

"My poor toes." Tina sits on the floor, pulls her boots off, and rubs her feet. "Hey, look under the bed."

You crouch down and see *Level Exit* carved on the flagstones.

"Great, let's get out of here," you say. "Give me a hand

moving the bed out of the way, guys."

It's a strangely heavy bed. Lumpy too. Together, you heave it to one side. The mattress clanks and tinkles as it hits the floor. Hmm, that's no ordinary mattress. You undo a row of buttons, and out fall two crowns, a bracelet and a diamond necklace, followed by a stream of gold coins.

Zim grins. "We got a huge reward after all."

Five minutes later, weighed down with treasure, you step onto the *Level Exit* flagstones, and…

Suddenly you're back in the real world, sitting at the table with Jim and Tina. *Bonus Level Completed* is in big sparkly letters on your laptop screen.

"We won!" Jim says. "That was cool. Wow, is that the time? I'd better get home for lunch. See you guys back here next Saturday to play Level 101." He folds up his laptop, grabs a walking stick and limps out the door, going step-thud-step-thud-step-thud.

"Um," you say to Tina. "Was Jim's foot always like that?"

She frowns. "Can't remember. It…must have been, right?"

You go to the window and look out. There's Jim, going step-thud-step-thud-step-thud along the pavement.

On the other side of the road is an old couple in their seventies, out for a stroll. They're both dressed in green and look familiar somehow. They see Jim, and the woman says something to the man. Reluctantly, he waves something twig-like. Jim's walking stick vanishes, and he walks away normally, not even noticing the magical change.

"You have weird neighbors," Tina says. "See you next week."

Congratulations, you've finished this part of your story. Then again, if you'd made different choices, things might have gone even better (or much worse). Have you gotten lost in the maze? Been attacked by the bone army? Run from the giant rolling head? Helped the extremely wet queen? Said hello to the Reverse Dragon? Avoided the Zenobian Snapper?

It's time to make a decision. Do you:

Go back to the beginning of the story and try another path? **P113**

Or

Go to the great big list of choices? **P118**

The Narrow Doorway

No, you don't trust Zim's Invisibility spell. Not enough to trust your life on it. (Or Zim and Tina's lives.)

You point to the narrow doorway. "We'll run there, one at a time, as quietly as possible."

They nod.

You go first. The doorway's only a dozen steps away, but it feels like running a mile. Luckily, the goblins don't notice you.

Crouched in the doorway's shadow, you turn back to the archway you came from. Zim and Tina are still behind the fallen statue, pushing and shoving each other and arguing in loud whispers. Idiots.

A goblin looks around, spots them and shrieks an alarm. They make a mad dash towards your doorway, chased by dozens of goblins.

"It's all her fault," Zim shouts.

"It's all his fault," Tina shouts, at the same time.

They're *still* arguing?

With the goblins in pursuit, you sprint along a twisty-turny corridor and through an open red door. Tina and Zim follow you, then you slam the door shut behind them. Just in time – seconds later, muffled pounding and kicking and screeching come from the other side.

"What sort of room is this?" Tina gasps, out of breath.

"Looks sort of steampunky."

True. The room's circular, with tarnished brass walls,

floor and ceiling, and is lit by gas lamps. No one's running around wearing goggles and a bowler hat and talking in a bad British accent though.

"What's holding that door shut?" Zim asks. "There's not even a handle or knob, let alone a lock or bolt."

"And no other exits." Tina draws her sword, clearly expecting the red door to burst open any moment. "It's a trap!" she adds in her Admiral Ackbar voice (which is pretty bad – her Chewbacca impersonation is much better).

You draw your bow. Zim pulls his wand from his robe.

From somewhere above comes a metallic clunk, followed by squeaking and whirring. The circular floor quivers under your feet, then rotates, while the walls spin in the opposite direction. Dizzy, you fall to your knees. What next? Will the ceiling descend and crush you? Will giant spinning saw blades come out of the walls?

A few seconds later, the spinning slows and stops with another clunk. The goblin noises have gone. The red door has vanished – instead, now there's a white door, a yellow door, and a purple door.

"I feel sick," Zim moans, lying on the floor. "That was worse than a roller coaster."

"You've never ridden a roller coaster," Tina snaps, getting back to her feet. "Riding a plastic horsey on a carousel with your seven-year-old brother doesn't count."

He sits up. "That horse was a public safety hazard! I complained to the manager!"

"Guys!" you interrupt. "Concentrate. Look, the doors

have changed. There's three now, and none of them are red."

"Impossible. Doors don't just appear from nowhere." Tina glares at them as if trying to scare them into disappearing. "This better not be one of those stupid magic mazes. I told you before, I hate mazes."

"Yeah, yeah, we know." Zim staggers to his feet and looks around the room. "No sign of magic, so it must be a *non*-magic maze. Better?"

She scowls at him.

"I reckon we're inside a giant mechanical puzzle," you say. "Perhaps it's a security system to guard a treasure room. Now we have to pick the right door to find the treasure and the level exit."

Tina sniffs. "And behind the other two doors are horrible gory deaths, no doubt."

Zim agrees with her. Those two agreeing on anything is a bad sign.

"There must be clues if we're smart enough to spot them," you insist. "Look there, a line of scraped red paint – that's probably from the red door that disappeared. And every yard or so, there's a vertical line that's scraped shiny. I think these walls are panels which slide up and down when the room spins, and some of the panels have doors in them. Make sense?"

Neither Tina nor Zim look like they believe you, but neither has any better suggestions.

You take a closer look at the three doors.

The white door is plain and smooth, and hums like a refrigerator. Maybe it really is a refrigerator, with milk cartons, eggs and carrots inside? Nah, that seems too weird even for this place.

The yellow door has a brass button at knee level. Below it, "Don't Press Me" is engraved in Dwarvish. If the door's for dwarves, why is it normal height? And why would anyone have a doorbell with a "Don't Press Me" sign?

The purple door is lined with rows of silver rivets shaped like little skulls. With fangs. Charming.

None of that's any help, but Zim and Tina are waiting for you to make a decision. Do you choose:

The white door? **P36**

Or

The yellow door? **P58**

Or

The purple door? **P59**

The White Door

"This way," you say, trying to sound confident, and open the white door. To your relief, it's not a refrigerator – that would have been so embarrassing – instead, it's another twisty corridor.

Three turns and two curves later, you all stop at another white door.

Tina opens it. Inside is an empty circular room, with brass walls, floor and ceiling. She sighs. "Surprise, surprise, another round room with a white door and a yellow door and a purple door. Have we doubled back to the same room, or are there a million identical rooms? Did I mention that I hate mazes?"

As soon as you walk in, the white door slams itself shut. From above comes a familiar clunk, followed by squeaking and whirring. For a few seconds, the circular floor spins one way while the walls spin the other way, just like last time.

Zim lies curled on the floor (again), groaning (again). "I'm dying. Dying, I tell you."

Tina looks around, then turns to you. "The room didn't change this time. There's still a white door, a purple door, and a yellow door."

You shake your head. "Before, it had a white door, a yellow door, and a purple door."

"Huh?"

"The same color doors, but their order's changed."

"Very observant, smarty pants. Doesn't help us, though.

If you're right about walls and doors sliding up and down when the room spins, then this might be the same room. Or not." She growls. "We can't even trust the door we came through. There could be a big bucket full of zombie piranha behind it now. Mazes aren't fair."

"Would you please stop telling us every five seconds how much you hate mazes?" Zim asks from the floor. "I'm going to–" Mid-sentence, he stops and stares at the purple door.

"Going to what?" Tina asks suspiciously. "Barf on the floor? Don't you dare. Use your wizard hat as a barf bag if you have to. Zim? Are you listening?"

Apparently not. He points at the purple door. "In the last room – actually I think we're still in the same room – I said there's no magic in here. True. But from down here, I can see a tiny gap under that door. Something's glowing violet through there, just like under the purple door in the last room. And through my Enchanted Shadow Crystal Lenses, the glow isn't just violet, it's ultra-violet."

"Violet, lavender, whatever," Tina says. "Who cares what shade of purple?"

"In this game, ultra-violet is a super-powerful magical color. As you'd know if you were a magic user like me." He checks around the room, especially under the other two doors. "Nope, no other magic. I think this is a clue – the same ultra-violet glow under a purple door, either in two rooms or the same room twice. It's the only thing we know definitely hasn't changed."

"Yeah," you say, "but not much of a clue by itself."

"Better than nothing." Tina strides towards the purple door.

"No, stop!" Zim shouts as he scrambles to his feet. "Ultra-violet is the color of necromancy."

"Necro Nancy?" She shrugs. "Never heard of her." She's lying – she just loves winding Zim up.

"Necromancy! Death magic!" he squeals.

Death magic sounds scary. Although Zim could be wrong – he's not the smartest wizard around. It's time to make a decision, and fast. Do you:

Stop Tina opening the purple door? **P39**

Or

Let her open the purple door? **P53**

Don't Open the Purple Door

"Tina, no!" you shout. "Zim's our magic expert. We have to trust him. Just like he and I trust you about warrior stuff. Please."

She stops, her hand an inch from the purple door, and glares at you both. For a moment, you think she's going to open it anyway just to be annoying, but then she sighs and drops her hand. "Okay, scaredy-cats. Which door – white or yellow? Anything to get out of this maze."

"Any other magical clues?" you ask Zim.

"No. Do the other doors look the same as they did before?"

"Exactly the same," Tina says.

"Yep," you say, looking around. "Hey, no, look at the label below the brass button on the yellow door. It has 'Press Me' engraved on it in Dwarvish. Before, it said, 'Don't Press Me'.

Zim crouches down and stares at the label. "So, this is a different room. Or a different door. Or it has a sneaky doorbell that can change labels, like James Bond's car license plates."

"Or Velzon can't read Dwarvish properly," Tina points out.

"Thanks," you say. Not that she could read one word of Dwarvish.

"So, it's your fault if you pick the wrong door now," she adds.

"Thanks again."

It's time to make a decision. Do you:

Pick the white door? **P41**

Or

Pick the yellow door? **P42**

The White Door

"Let's try the white door," you say.

Zim and Tina grunt unenthusiastically, but follow you through it.

Three turns and two curves later, you stop at another white door. Inside is an empty circular room, with brass walls, floor and ceiling, and a white door and a yellow door and a purple door. Exactly like the last one. Sigh.

As soon as you walk in, the white door slams itself shut. There are the usual noises, then the circular floor spins one way while the walls spin the other way. Just like last time.

"I hate mazes," Tina grumbles.

"We know," Zim grumbles. "I hate spinning rooms."

"We know."

"Let's get out of here," you say. "Any ideas?"

Nope. They've both given up.

You check all three doors, but they look the same as last time. The label below the brass button on the yellow door reads "Press Me."

It's time to make a decision. Do you open:

The white door? **P41**

Or

The yellow door? **P42**

Or

The purple door? **P59**

The Yellow Door

"Okay then, the yellow door." You try to open it, but it won't budge.

Zim leans over and presses the "Press Me" doorbell.

"Good thinking," you tell him, embarrassed at not thinking of that yourself.

Something behind the door clicks and whirs. "Not more spinning," Zim groans, and slumps to the floor.

But the floor doesn't move.

You'd expected the yellow door would open. Instead, a much smaller yellow door – not much taller than your knees – opens inside it.

"Maybe it's a doggy door," says Tina.

"With a doorbell?" you ask.

"Dogs are smart enough to use doorbells."

"Not smart enough to read Dwarvish, though."

"Isn't it more likely to be a dwarf-sized door, built by dwarves, so that dwarves can read the doorbell label, press the doorbell, then walk through the dwarf-sized door?" Zim asks.

Tina rolls her eyes. "Wow, listen to Mister Sensible."

"Good one again, Zim." You're embarrassed at not thinking of this either. "So, I guess we have to crawl through?"

As the three of you get down on your knees and peer through the small yellow door, a grumpy dwarf appears, holding an axe. "Mmmph. Thought you might be goblins for a moment."

"No, sir," Tina says.

"I'm a woman!"

"Sorry, ma'am. Nice beard."

"Mmmph. You're late. Well, don't stand around cluttering up the place. Come in."

Late for what? "Thank you, ma'am," you say, afraid to ask. Never make a dwarf angry, especially when she's holding an axe.

"And close that door," she says. "There's an awful cold draft out there sometimes."

The three of you squeeze through the small yellow door, closing it behind you, and follow the dwarf down a corridor. The corridor's dwarf-height, so she can walk fine, but you have to keep crawling.

Nice corridor otherwise. The walls are blue stone, intricately carved with runes and bearded faces. Probably this dwarf clan's ancestors from the last thousand or so years.

"Magnificent stonework, ma'am," you say, partly to be polite and partly because it's true.

"Mmmph."

"My hands and knees are getting sore," whispers Tina.

"Shush," Zim whispers back.

The dwarf overheard. "Ceiling not high enough for you, missy? I can fix that in a jiffy – come here and I'll chop your legs off." She roars with laughter.

That's a very old dwarf joke, probably older than this

corridor. You all pretend to laugh.

To your relief, the next door (carved with more runes and bearded faces) leads to a larger room with a ceiling high enough to let you stand, although Zim has to carry his tall wizard hat.

A dozen worried-looking dwarves line the room. They stare at you, frown, and mutter to each other.

"Is that them?" one asks.

"Must be. They don't look the type, do they? Won't last five minutes."

"Well, they can't do any worse than the last lot, can they?"

And so on. You glance at Tina and Zim, who shrug.

The female dwarf leads you onwards. The next door is even grander – polished oak, inlaid with strips of gold, spelling out the clan name Grash'klrgl.

She waves you through the door.

Wow. It's a throne room, the most magnificent room in any dwarf citadel, and normally only seen by honored guests. In your years of gaming, you've never seen one so luxurious, with stone pillars that glitter like opals, and furniture of oak and precious metals, sparkling with gemstones. On a high marble platform with steps on three sides is a throne of turquoise and silver, topped with a pearl-like jewel the size of a football.

Something's wrong, though. Where is everyone? Looks like they left in a hurry, too. Furniture's been knocked over, and a goblet's lying on the floor in a puddle of wine.

"Mmmph. Best of luck." The dwarf leaves, locking the

three of you inside.

"Um, I'm confused. What's happening?" Zim puts his hat on and looks around.

"There's only one logical explanation," Tina says. "They think we're the three glorious tall emperors foretold by ancient dwarven prophecy. Any moment now, they'll be back with our coronation feast of spicy fried chicken, strawberry smoothies, and chocolate brownies dipped in chocolate sauce."

"Did you just make that up?" you ask.

"Yup. Good, wasn't it?"

"Makes as much sense as anything I can think of. We're missing something important. Why would dwarves invite us in, then lock us in their throne room surrounded by their treasure?"

"What's that?" Zim points across the room.

Huh? Sticking out of the stone floor is a grey triangular wedge. It glides along the floor, occasionally bumping into furniture, then turns, sinks down into the floor and disappears. A few seconds later, it reappears, and circles the marble throne platform. Oh, that's no wedge, it's a fin.

"Stone shark!" all three of you say at the same time.

Zim looks at you in astonishment. "How do you two know about stone sharks?"

"We elves know and respect elemental creatures," you say. "Especially really dangerous ones like stone sharks — them, we prefer to respect from a distance."

"I read this cool graphic novel where an evil queen used

stone sharks to destroy her enemy's fortress," Tina says. "Great plan, until the sharks accidentally crushed her to death during her victory parade. Stone sharks are totally bad-ass. No one tells them what to do."

"Only senior lithomancers can control them," Zim says. "And before anyone asks, no, I'm not even a junior lithomancer. All the advice I've read about stone sharks says to hide somewhere far from any stone and hope they'll swim away." He climbs onto a wooden table – not that that would be much protection.

The stone shark shows no interest in him or anyone else, but also doesn't look like it's about to swim away. It circles the marble throne platform again, "swimming" through the stone floor like a normal shark through water.

"I think it wants something from the platform." You look up the marble steps to the throne. "Food, maybe? What do they eat? Gems?"

Tina shakes her head. "There are gems everywhere in this room. The shark's not gobbling them up."

"What about that giant pearl thingy over the throne? If it is a pearl. It doesn't look like any I've ever seen. Not that I'm an expert on giant pearls."

"Oh. Mmm. Yes." Zim runs back to the door, and knocks. "Excuse me, dwarves. That huge pearly gem on top of your throne – did you dig it up recently?"

"Yes, the Moonstone was unearthed just six days ago, in our new Krlb'zgrb mine," comes the female dwarf's muffled voice through the door. "It is our finest treasure. No other clan has anything to match it."

"And did the stone shark appear soon afterwards?"

"Mmmph."

Zim looks smug. "That pearly gem isn't a gem. It's a stone shark's egg, and the shark wants it back."

"Then kill the shark! What kind of magical pest exterminators are you?" she snaps.

Oh, perhaps she invited you in by mistake?

"We're not exterminators," you say. "We never said we were."

"Mmmmmph."

The dwarves argue amongst themselves. The door's too thick for you to hear their words, but they sound angry. With each other, or with you?

"The only way out of this room is through that door," you whisper to Tina and Zim, "so we have to get the dwarves to open it. First, we need a bargaining chip to stop them killing us."

After dodging the stone shark, you lead Zim and Tina up the marble platform and onto the throne. Removing the egg from its silver mounting is hard work, even using your dagger as a lever. Tina helps with the point of her sword. The egg unexpectedly pops free, and bounces on a step before Zim catches it.

"I hope you know what you're doing, Velzon." He hands the heavy egg back to you.

"So do I. You guys ready?"

They nod. Tina draws her sword and Zim raises his wand.

"Okay, let's give the shark its egg back," you say, loudly so the dwarves will hear.

As hoped, the door opens. A dozen heavily armed dwarves rush in, but stop when they see the egg in your arms.

"Give that back now," growls the largest dwarf, twirling axes in both hands.

It's time to make a decision. Do you:

Distract the dwarves by throwing them the egg? **P49**

Or

Throw the egg to the stone shark? **P51**

Throw the egg to the Dwarves

"Sure," you tell the dwarves. "Catch it if you can."

You toss the egg down the steps to your left, not directly towards the dwarves. As you'd hoped, it bounces unpredictably, and the dwarves chase after it. Meanwhile, the three of you race down the other side of the throne platform, heading for the open door.

It was never a great plan, just the best you could think of at the time. And it almost works…until two snarling dwarves block your path. They raise their throwing axes, but are interrupted by shouting and screaming from other dwarves.

A dwarf runs past, holding the egg, but is hit by a grey blur – the stone shark – and becomes a long red bloodstain. The egg bounces twice, is caught by one terrified-looking dwarf who quickly tosses it to another, who in turn tries outrunning the shark, unsuccessfully. The egg bounces away again. The enraged shark headbutts a stone pillar, then the throne platform, which both creak and collapse into rubble. You can't see the egg any more, and apparently neither can the dwarves – they're running in all directions. Hopefully they've forgotten about you.

"Let's get out of here before the shark destroys the whole place!" Tina drags you towards the door.

"Where's Zim?"

She points back to where Zim lies on the floor, a dwarf axe in his head. "We have to go, now!"

The shark rams a wall, huge granite blocks tumble all around, and everything turns black.

Suddenly you're all back in the real world, sitting at the kitchen table. On your laptop screen are the words *Game Over*.

"I've got a splitting headache," Jim says, rubbing his forehead. "What were we playing? I can't remember a thing."

Tina shrugs. "Something about eggs? No, that doesn't sound right."

"I'm sure there was a shark," you say. "Fairly sure. It's all fading. Hey, does anyone else have sore knees?"

Sorry, this part of your story is over. If you'd made different choices, things might have gone better (or even worse). Have you met the Emerald Sage? Been attacked by the bone army? Run from the giant rolling head? Helped the extremely wet queen? Said hello to the Reverse Dragon? Avoided the Zenobian Snapper?

It's time to make a decision. Do you:

Go back to the previous section? **P42**

Or

Go back to the beginning of the story and try another path? **P113**

Or

Go to the great big list of choices? **P118**

Throw the egg to the Shark

The dwarves don't have any right to steal the stone shark's egg. It's not a jewel, no matter how pretty it looks.

Hoping this isn't a huge mistake, you wait for the stone shark to glide back into view, then toss the egg towards it.

Stone sharks are eyeless, but somehow it senses the approaching egg. It changes direction, leaps into the air and swallows the egg whole, then disappears into the floor.

"Just like I said, you can't trust elves and humans. Kill them!" yells the largest dwarf, and raises the axes in his (or her) hands.

"Look!" Zim points to the throne's seat, where the words *Level Exit* have suddenly appeared.

An axe flashes past your head. Ouch, what happened? You reach up and discover half your left ear is gone. Tina collapses with an axe in her helmet, and Zim's bleeding too – he's lost two fingers. You and he drag Tina onto the throne, and–

Suddenly you're back in the real world, sitting at the kitchen table, staring at the words *Bonus Level Completed* on your laptop screen.

"I've got a splitting headache." Tina rubs her unmarked forehead. "My knees hurt too. I'm out of here."

"My knees hurt, and my hand hurts." Jim counts his fingers carefully.

"My pointy left ear hurts," you say. "As well as my

knees."

"You don't have pointy ears."

"Um, yeah, right. What were we playing? I can't remember a thing about it. Something about knees and eggs? Doesn't make sense."

He shrugs. "See you next week. I'm going home to feed my fish. Don't know why I just thought of that."

Congratulations, you've finished this part of your story. Then again, if you'd made different choices, things might have gone even better (or much worse). Have you met the Emerald Sage? Been attacked by the bone army? Run from the giant rolling head? Helped the extremely wet queen? Said hello to the Reverse Dragon? Avoided the Zenobian Snapper?

It's time to make a decision. Do you:

Would you like to:

Go back to the beginning of the story and try another path? **P113**

Or

Go to the great big list of choices? **P118**

The Purple Door

"Okay, scaredy-cats, here goes." Her sword at the ready, Tina tugs the purple door open.

You draw your bow.

"We're going to die," Zim whimpers, raising his wand.

There's an icy blast of air from the other side of the door, but nothing horrible leaps out.

"It's just a purple floor covered in dusty old bones." Tina sounds disappointed.

"Ultra-violet, not purple," Zim corrects. "But you can't see that without Enchanted Shadow Crystal Lenses."

"Whatever. So then, use your super magic sunglasses and tell us what nasties are waiting in there."

"No idea, coz the whole floor is glowing ultra-violet. That could mean we drop dead the moment we step in. Or there could be dozens of monsters hiding amongst the bones. Or it could mean the room's harmless, and some necromancer's favorite interior decorating color is ultra-violet. Us magicians are weird."

"Yeah, I've noticed." Tina pokes her sword and then a foot through the doorway. Nothing happens.

"There's a door in the far corner." You point. "See it? The black door in the black frame, with the black symbols carved in it."

She peers across the room. "Where?"

Zim can't see it either, until he casts an Owl Sight spell on his Crystal Lenses. "Good spotting, Velzon. Must be your elven eyes. That's not just any old door, that's a Sanctuary Portal, like we found back on Level 44."

"I remember that." Tina grins. "Sanctuary Portals are awesome! Full restore of health points and armor points. That's bound to be the level exit too."

"Probably," Zim says. "If we can get to it without getting killed. This will take careful planning."

Too late. Tina's already jogging across the room, kicking bones aside as she goes.

"We'd better help her," you tell Zim.

"So much for careful planning," he grumbles, following you into the room.

Wow, it's cold in here. Like a walk-in freezer.

"Slow down," you call to Tina.

Surprisingly, she does, and turns back, frowning. "As well as a million dusty broken skeletons, there are also a zillion or so broken weapons and rags. I'm guessing they're from the last million people to try to walk through here, so, um…yeah, let's play safe and do this together. What's your plan, Zim?"

"Plan? What plan?" He mutters, points his wand in various directions, and shrugs. "The only thing I'm sure of is that we three are the only living creatures in here. And I'm cold."

"Join us," whisper hundreds of voices around you. Bones twitch and rattle, then rise and connect to form nightmarish mutant skeletons – some two-skulled or three-legged, some walking on six arms, some crawling like giant snakes on dozens of human ribcages. They all have glowing violet eyes. "Join us forever."

"Run for the portal!" you yell.

Tina takes the lead, swinging her sword at skeletons that come too close.

They shatter and fall. More quickly replace them.

Zim zaps skeletons with his wand, but the death magic is too strong – they just stagger and pause, before resuming a zombie-like march towards you.

Your arrows whoosh harmlessly through skeletons' ribcages. You karate-kick a three-headed skeleton as it reaches out a bony hand, and run faster, dodging anything that moves.

The Sanctuary Portal is close now, mostly thanks to Tina smiting skeletons out of the way.

Thousands of bones rattle, dance into the air, and form a hideous octopus-shaped bone monster as tall as the ceiling. "Join us," it whispers.

Tina lops off one bony tentacle, but is knocked to the floor by another.

"Your mortal blades and arrows cannot kill me," the monster whispers.

Okay, that gives you an idea. You grab a long straight bone from the floor, and shoot it like an arrow into the monster's glowing eye, hoping that death magic can be hurt by more death magic.

It works – sort of. The monster shrieks and collapses, thrashing its tentacles.

"Run for your lives!" you yell, sure this is your final chance.

You dodge a dozen snapping jaws, stomp on one bony tentacle, and stumble the last few steps to the warmth and safety of the Sanctuary Portal.

Someone screams. You whirl around. Zim and Tina are dangling from the monster's tentacles.

"No!" you scream.

In a flash of violet light, they both turn to skeletons, and fall to the floor amongst the millions of other bones.

Level Exit appears on the Portal's floor under your feet. Suddenly you're back in the real world, sitting at the kitchen table and shivering, staring at the words *Game Over* on your laptop screen.

You're alone, but weren't you playing with...um, a wizard and warrior? They saved you, didn't they? What were their names? It's fading fast, like waking after a nightmare. Something about a skeleton octopus? No, that doesn't make sense, octopuses don't have skeletons. Maybe you imagined the whole thing.

Onscreen, words flicker. *Dungeon of Doom. Game Over. Try again?*

Again? You don't remember playing it at all.

Congratulations, you've finished this part of your story. Then again, if you'd made different choices, things might have gone much better (or much worse). Have you met the Emerald Sage? Run from the giant rolling head? Helped the extremely wet queen? Said hello to the Reverse Dragon? Avoided the Zenobian Snapper?

It's time to make a decision. Do you:

Go back to the beginning of the story and try another path? **P113**

Or

Go to the great big list of choices? **P118**

The Yellow Door

"Okay, let's open the yellow door," you say. But when you try, it doesn't budge, not even when the three of you try together.

Zim presses the "Don't Press Me" doorbell.

"Can't you read?" shouts an angry voice in Dwarvish from somewhere inside.

"Sorry," he says back.

"We could smash the door down," Tina suggests.

"How? Using your head as a battering ram?" Zim asks.

"This must be a dead end," you say hurriedly, before they can start another argument. "Let's try another door."

It's time to make a decision. Do you open:

The white door? **P41**

Or

The purple door? **P59**

The Purple Door

"Let's try the purple door." You try not to worry about its rows of silver rivets shaped like skulls. After all, lots of things in dungeons have skulls on them. Wallpaper, toothbrushes, teddy bears probably. It's traditional. Old school.

You pull the heavy purple door open. An icy blast of air blows into your face.

"Whoop-de-do. A big empty room with a purple floor covered in dusty old bones." Tina sounds disappointed.

"Urp." Zim peers through his Enchanted Shadow Crystal Lenses. "That's not purple, it's ultra-violet. The color of necromancy."

"Necro Nancy? Never heard of her."

She's joking. A month ago, she complained about "neck romance" just to annoy him.

Zim falls for it, again. "Necromancy! Death magic! That whole room's incredibly dangerous."

Tina smirks.

The cold air stops blowing and starts sucking instead.

"That's quite an air conditioner they've got in there," she says.

"It could be a huge monster breathing in and out?" you say.

"Someone or something could be trying to suck us in there," Zim says. "We should stand back, just in case."

Tina grins nervously. "Nah, I agree with Velzon – it's a

humungous monster doing some heavy breathing. Hopefully a gigantic ice dragon, guarding an even more gigantic horde of diamonds. We'll wait until we hear snoring, then sneak in and steal the lot."

The sucky breeze becomes a sucky wind. Her grin disappears and she takes a step back.

"Let's close the door," you say.

But the open door won't budge an inch, not even with the three of you pushing and pulling it.

The white and yellow doors blow open, and the sucky wind becomes a sucky hurricane. Two squealing goblins blow past and vanish into the room.

"It's a Deadly Doom Vortex," Zim yells over the howling gale. "Hang on for your lives!"

Great advice, except there's nothing to hang on to. Within seconds, all three of you are pulled off your feet and sucked into the room.

The wind stops, the purple door slams shut, and you fall to the floor.

"Ow," Tina says. "Skeletons are terrible landing pads. Wow, it's really cold in here."

"We're doomed," says Zim.

The floor's almost hidden beneath millions of bones, presumably from everyone who's ever died in here. Humans, elves, dwarves, trolls, even a couple of suspiciously new goblin skeletons a few yards away.

"Join us," whisper hundreds of icy voices around the room. Thousands of bones rattle and connect into nightmarish mutant skeletons with too many heads or limbs. Their skulls' empty eye sockets glow purple. "Join us forever," their voices whisper.

"No, thanks." Tina beheads a skeleton with her sword before it can grab her.

Zim waves his wand and zaps a few skeletons. They don't fall, just stagger then resume a zombie-like march towards you.

Your arrows are useless, whooshing through skeletons' ribcages. How are you supposed to kill something already dead?

The three of you fight back to back, but are surrounded. The last thing you see is an eight-tentacled bone monster looming over you, then a flash of icy violet light.

Suddenly you're all back in the real world, sitting at the kitchen table and shivering. The words *Game Over* sparkle on your laptop screen.

Tina hugs herself. "Why is it so cold in here? What happened?"

"Weren't we playing a computer game?" Zim asks. "Something about a giant purple octopus skeleton?"

"Something like that, I think," you say. "No, that can't be right. Octopuses don't have skeletons."

"Stupid game, whatever it was. See you guys next week." Tina leaves, carefully walking around the purple rug on the floor.

Sorry, this part of your story is over. If you'd made different choices, things might have gone much better (or even worse).

Have you met the Emerald Sage? Run from the giant rolling head? Helped the extremely wet queen? Said hello to the Reverse Dragon? Avoided the Zenobian Snapper?

It's time to make a decision. Do you:

Go back to the previous section? **P32**

Or

Go back to the beginning of the story and try another path? **P113**

Or

Go to the great big list of choices? **P118**

Ogres, Rock and Roll

You turn right, towards the ogres. Sure, ogres are scary, but they're also dim and predictable.

The three of you advance down the corridor, passing several closed doors.

The ogres' footsteps get closer, echoing down the corridor.

You stop and listen. "Four, maybe five of them, around the next corner. Get ready."

Tina raises her sword. Zim summons a sparkly green fireball. You draw an arrow from your quiver and raise your bow.

Four huge ogres burst around the corner and…thunder straight past.

"They didn't even notice us," Tina grumbles. "How rude."

"One stepped on my foot," Zim says. "Ouchies."

"Maybe they were running from something," you say.

"Like what?"

"Something worse than four ogres. So maybe we should run too."

Zim and Tina aren't convinced, until a head rolls around the corner – a head as wide as the corridor and nearly touching the ceiling. It rolls straight towards you, grinning and waggling a long purple tongue.

"Run!" You take off down the corridor, not checking whether Zim and Tina are following. Well, they told you to lead the way, right?

The first door you reach is locked, and there's no time to try your elven lock-picking skills.

The next one's locked too. And the one after that.

Finally, gasping for breath, you reach an open doorway, but inside is pitch black.

You glance back. Zim and Tina are close behind. Close behind them is the rolling head.

It's time to make a decision, and fast. Do you:

Enter the dark room? **P65**

Or

Keep running? **P100**

Dark Room

You run into the dark room, and immediately hit a wall. "Ow!"

Tina and Zim run into your back.

"Double ow!"

The ceiling starts to glow, revealing that the room's only a few feet deep and wide.

"Stupid elf! This is a dead end!" Tina snarls.

Outside, the giant head rolls to a stop. Luckily, it's too big to fit through the doorway, but its long purple tongue snakes out, grabs your leg and pulls. The room's metal door starts to slide closed by itself – no idea why, but a door between you and that giant head sounds great.

The door hits the tongue, and stops.

"Stab it!" Tina shouts.

You draw your dagger from your belt.

"No, tickle it! Trust me, Velzon!" Zim shouts.

It's time to make a decision. Do you:

Stab the tongue? **P66**

Or

Tickle the tongue? **P68**

Stabby Stabby

You stab the purple tongue.

Its end falls off, and the room's door slides closed. Outside, the giant head roars in pain or rage or both. It batters at the door, but can't get through.

The tongue end stretches and swells and keeps growing, thicker and longer, like a large snake. Tina stabs it with her sword, but that just makes more bits fall off, and they grow into more snakes.

"I told you not to stab it," Zim moans. "It's Orzkedryle's Endless Legion of Tongue Serpents. We're doomed."

"Orzka what?"

Dozens of tongue serpents wrap around the three of you, squeezing, crushing.

With your last breath, you scream, not that it helps. Everything turns black, and...

Suddenly the three of you are back in the kitchen, wrapped together in a pile on the floor.

"Gross!" you say, and Tina says "Blurgh!" and Jim says, "No one's allowed to cuddle me except Mom," all at the same time.

Blushing, you look at each other, then stare at the floor.

"I'm late for lunch. Bye." Jim grabs his laptop and rushes out the door.

"I'm late for...something too." Tina leaves, almost running.

You stare at your laptop screen. *Game Over. Try Again?*

Sorry, this part of your story is over. If you'd made different choices, things might have gone better (or even worse).

Have you met the Emerald Sage? Gotten lost in the maze? Been attacked by the bone army? Helped the extremely wet queen? Said hello to the Reverse Dragon? Avoided the Zenobian Snapper?

It's time to make a decision. Do you:

Go back to the previous section? **P65**

Or

Go back to the beginning of the story and try another path? **P113**

Or

Go to the great big list of choices? **P118**

Tickly Tickly

Feeling silly, you tickle the purple tongue. The giant head giggles, then roars helplessly with laughter. It laughs so hard that its tongue loosens its hold on your leg. You push the tongue back out of the room, and the door slides shut.

"How did you know that tickling would work?" you ask Zim. "Is that some sort of wizardly secret magic trick?"

He looks embarrassed. "Um, not really. That head out there is the infamous Orzkedryle and her Endless Legion of Tongue Serpents, and I've heard she's unbeatable in combat. But…my tongue's ticklish, so I thought maybe her tongue would be too."

"How do you know your tongue's ticklish?" Tina asks.

"Haven't you ever tickled your tongue?"

"No! What kind of weirdo are you?"

"The kind who's just saved our lives," you point out.

She scowls. "Maybe, maybe not. We're still trapped in this stupid tiny little room."

You look at the mysteriously glowing ceiling, the sliding metal door, and a row of dwarven runes next to the door. Oh. "I don't think this is really a room."

"Then what is it? A chocolate cake?"

You press one of the runes. As you'd suspected, the whole room quivers and hums and starts to move.

Zim squeals. "It's a trash compactor, like in Star Wars. We'll be crushed to death!"

"The whole room's moving – this is an elevator," you say.

"You watch too many movies."

Tina snorts. "An elevator in a dungeon? Don't be ridic—"

The door opens, revealing...no giant head, to your relief. Just an empty stone-walled corridor, dimly lit by thousands of glowing blue dots on the walls.

"Lucky guess," she mutters.

The three of you step out, and immediately bang your heads on the low ceiling.

"Looks like a dwarven mine tunnel." Zim rubs the top of his head and picks his tall wizard hat off the floor. "I don't mind dwarves, except they're too short."

"Well, yeah, but if they were taller then they wouldn't be dwarves," Tina says. "What are these little blue glowing thingies?"

"Slumberworms," you say. "Don't touch them."

"Poisonous?"

"One bite sends you to sleep in seconds."

"Doesn't sound so bad."

"While you're asleep, the worms eat you alive."

"Gross!" She steps back. "Okay, worm nerd, which way do we go to get away from them?"

You look and listen and sniff again in both directions. "Less worms if we go left, but only because it's cold and damp. They don't like cold and damp."

"There's strong magic that way too, I can feel it," Zim adds. "Can't tell what it is."

"To the right is warmer, and I see a faint golden glow," you continue. "Fire, maybe, but I don't smell smoke. And I don't smell dwarves in either direction – dunno where they've gone."

"Let's go right," Tina says.

"Let's go left," says Zim.

Sigh. It's time to make a decision. Do you:

Go left, towards the cold and damp? **P71**

Or

Go right, towards the warm glow? **P89**

So Cool

The three of you turn left. The corridor floor slopes downwards, occasionally passing empty rooms. Around a corner, a wide puddle blocks the corridor, and moisture glistens on the walls and drips from the ceiling. On the far side of the puddle, the floor slopes upwards again.

"Why are we stopping?" Tina asks. "It's only a puddle of water. Isn't it?"

Zim chews his lip and squints through his Enchanted Shadow Crystal Lenses. "Water, sure, but…there's something else here too. Something magical. And powerful. What do you think, Velzon?"

You shrug, equally puzzled. "Yeah, my pointy elven ears are twitching. There's elemental magic close by. Don't know exactly what or where, though."

Tina pokes her sword into the puddle, and taps the stone floor below. "Maybe you two are scared of a puddle, but I'm not. It's too wide to jump over, and I'd rather not get my feet wet – that's all that bothers me. Zim, could you magic us up some rubber boots, or fly us over the puddle or something?"

He shakes his head. "The magical something is suppressing my wizardly powers. This might be a trap."

Tina pokes the puddle again with her sword, and then with the toe of her boot. Nothing happens again. She takes a few steps back, runs through the puddle, then turns and pokes her tongue out. "Come on, you big babies."

You follow her through the puddle. Your feet get wet too – elven boots aren't any more waterproof than warrior princess boots – but nothing else happens.

Zim frowns. "My mom says never to walk in wet shoes or you'll get blisters."

Tina snorts. "This is a dungeon. Blisters are the least of our problems. Don't worry, I promise I won't tell your mommy."

Grimacing and muttering to himself, Zim wades through the puddle, then the three of you squelch up the corridor.

"My left heel's getting a blister already," Zim whines.

"You'll feel much better after a nice warm bath," says a cheerful voice.

The three of you stop and look around, but see no one.

"Who said that?" you ask.

"It is I, Queen Moist, beloved ruler of the water spirits. Thank you, brave heroes, for rescuing me from that horrid puddle."

"You're a queen?" Tina asks. "I'm royalty too – Tina Warrior Princess. Pleased to meet you."

"Mmm." The queen doesn't sound impressed.

"Sorry to interrupt your royal majesty, but…are the three of us carrying you in our wet boots, Queen Moist?" Zim asks, staring suspiciously at his feet.

"Of course, we water spirits don't have silly boring bodies like you. We can live in any water. I wasted half an hour last week ordering a rat to rescue me from that puddle, but rodents are so stupid. You three look much cleverer."

"Thanks," Tina says.

"Forward!" orders the queen. "I must return to my palace immediately. My adoring subjects will be frantic with worry."

You, Tina and Zim look at each other.

"Is there a reward, your majesty?" You remember playing Level 84 a few weeks ago – after the three of you rescued a prince from a dragon, his grateful parents rewarded you with an enchanted carrot to get past the end-of-level giant rabbit.

"You will have my eternal royal gratitude," she says. "And as I said before, a nice warm bath."

"Oh." Whoop-de-do.

"And all the gold you can carry," she adds. "We'll be glad to get rid of it. We don't have much use for metal."

Oooh, gold, lots of gold. You, Tina and Zim look at each other again, and nod.

"Okay, your majesty, we'll take you home."

You continue squelching up the corridor. Wet boots are horrible to walk in. Zim (and his mom) might be right about blisters.

"It's not far," the queen says. "Next left, up the stairs, past the wall of screaming skulls, around the corner and second doorway on the right."

Wall of screaming skulls?

A few minutes later, you discover it's an actual wall made of hundreds and hundreds of skulls, all screaming at each other nonstop.

"Bone-face!"

"You're skinny!"

"Your nose has fallen off!"

"So has yours! And your eyeballs!"

"Don't you bare your teeth at me, cheeky!"

And so on, endlessly, shrieking at the top of their skeletal voices. They don't even notice you passing by.

"Such dreadful neighbors," Queen Moist says, as you turn a corner and their voices fade a little. "Always screaming, day and night. That's why my loyal subjects sent me on a special mission to find us a quieter new home."

"And did you?" Zim asks.

"No, I got stuck in that boring puddle. Blah, who'd want to live there?"

Ahead, more voices echo along the corridor. These ones are laughing and chattering. A wall of happy skulls? Probably not.

"Hear that? My loyal subjects must have heard news of my rescue," the queen continues. "And now they're preparing a surprise welcome-back party to show how much they adore me. How lovely."

A surprise party? Seems unlikely, but admittedly, you've never been to a water spirit party.

"Did you say second doorway on the right?" Tina asks. "There are no more doorways, just that little hole."

"That's the entrance to my royal palace. Hmm, you're big lumpy creatures – do you think you can squeeze through?"

You crouch down and peer through the narrow waist-high hole where the happy voices are coming from. On the other side is a wide stretch of water like a swimming pool, its surface rippling and splashing as if full of swimmers having fun. Invisible swimmers, that is. Oh, water spirits' bodies must be made of water.

Although maybe it's not a swimming pool. The water looks too deep, and…why so many bubbles? There's a weird soapy smell too. "We can fit through the hole. It doesn't look dangerous, but—"

"Dangerous?" The queen sounds insulted. "Of course it's not dangerous. You're my honored royal guests. Hurry up and take me through, that's an order. I'm queen, so you must obey me. That includes you, Princess Tina, because queens outrank princesses."

Tina rolls her eyes.

Zim shrugs. "Let's drop off Moist, collect the reward, and get out of here. Anything to be out of these wet boots."

A good plan, except…why's the queen's so bossy? Can you really trust her?

It's time to make a decision. Do you:

Go through the hole to the 'swimming pool'? **P76**

Or

No way, this must be a trap. **P86**

Swimming Pool (or is it?)

The three of you crawl through the hole and onto a wide white ledge at the water's edge.

This swimming pool, if that's what it is, is the biggest you've ever seen.

Hey, why are the ends rounded, and… no, unbelievable, are they…taps? This is no swimming pool, it's a giant bathtub! Hmm, where's the giant?

The water spirits see you, and suddenly stop laughing and chattering and splashing. The surface of the tub water goes still.

You feel Queen Moist wiggle out of your boots.

She splashes into the water. "Greetings, my adoring loyal subjects. I have returned safely. Let the celebrations begin!"

But celebrations don't begin. Instead there's silence, so quiet that you can hear the screaming skulls down the corridor.

The water ripples, and lots of voices start talking at once.

"I thought we'd finally got rid of her."

"You said she'd never find her way back!"

"I'm not putting up with her again."

"Should have boiled her into steam. That's the only way to get rid of unwanted royals."

"How dare you?" the queen snaps. "Royal guards, arrest these traitors immediately!"

"We are your royal guard, your royal snobbiness, or rather, we *were*. After we tricked you into leaving, we voted to become a democracy, so you're no longer queen, and you can go stick your—"

"Excuse me," interrupts Tina. "Terribly sorry, I can see you guys are really busy, so if we could just collect our reward, then we'll be on our way."

"What reward?" asks a grumpy voice from in the water.

"The queen promised us all the gold we can carry."

"Well, um, yes." The ex-queen sounds embarrassed. "And far more importantly, my eternal gratitude and a nice warm bath."

"Queeny tricked you," says the grumpy voice. "The only gold around here is those taps. If you can carry them, then sure, take them."

The water spirits roar with laughter.

The golden taps at the end of the bathtub are taller than you. Even if you could somehow get them off the wall, it would take a dozen trolls to lift even one of them.

"Let's get out of here," you tell Zim and Tina.

"No, please, two-legs, stay for your nice warm bath," the grumpy voice sneers. "Stay forever, we're so grateful."

Hundreds of water spirits hurl themselves at you. They're only water and don't hurt – it's like getting soaked by a horizontal rainstorm. Together, you, Tina and Zim inch backwards to the hole you came through. Slowly and carefully, because the ledge of the bathtub is now wet and slippery.

Zim's foot skids, and he nearly falls. He reaches out to you. "Help!"

Quickly now, do you:

Help Zim? **P79**

Or

No, you're not brave enough? **P84**

Help Zim

You grab Zim's hand to save him. Unfortunately, he grabs at Tina and she loses her balance too, and you all fall into the bathtub water together.

Your wet clothes and weapons drag you down. Zim, who can't swim, flails helplessly. Tina's normally a great swimmer, but she's weighed down by her steel armor and weapons.

Far below, an enormous chain glints in the water. Oh, of course, this is a bathtub, so that must be the chain for the plug. Just maybe it's also a way out of here.

You point down at the chain, and Tina nods. Zim's in bad shape, coughing and spluttering. You grab him and hold his head above water. "Take a deep breath," you tell him. "The only way out is down."

Looking confused, he nods.

After you all take a few lungfuls of air, you dive, towing him.

As hoped, at the bottom of the chain is a huge plug, wider than you are tall. You jam your dagger in one side of the plug and Tina jams her sword in the other side, together trying to lever it out of the plughole. It's hard work, and you're running out of breath fast. Zim's eyes are closed, and he looks half-dead.

At last, the plug jerks upwards, and bathwater pours down the plughole, washing you with it.

Down you go, through dark pipes, occasionally passing

glowing eyes and grasping tentacles. At least you can catch a breath now and again, although some of the awful smells make you cough and choke.

Finally, the current slows in a dimly lit cavern. Battered and bruised, you crawl onto a low stone ledge at the water's edge.

Where are Tina and Zim?

Is that Tina's cloak floating past? You grab it, and her hand grabs you.

"Help," she cries weakly.

You pull her out, wondering why she's so heavy, then discover she's still holding on to Zim.

"Is he dead?"

"Yes," Zim croaks, and coughs up some water. "Worse than dead."

The three of you rest for a while.

Until you hear something in the distance. "Rats, coming this way. Lots of them."

Tina shrugs. "So what? I'm not afraid of rats, even without my sword."

"We were in a giant bathtub, then washed down a giant sewer, so maybe they're giant rats? I lost my bow and dagger."

"My wand's broken," Zim says. "I lost my magic potions and my Big Book of Spells, and my magic sunglasses."

"Hah! I knew they were just sunglasses," Tina says.

"*Magic* sunglasses."

While they argue, you look around. The only doorway is

in the direction the rats are coming from. Back into the stinky water? No thanks, not if there's any alternative.

The wall on the other side of the ledge is covered in carvings, including a picture of three adventurers fighting off giant rats — someone's idea of a joke? Not funny. There's also a huge carved face with a creepy smile, and "Say the Magic Word!" carved on its forehead. Another unfunny joke? Or…

"Zim, is that a magic door?"

He nods. "Standard wizardly protection, sealed with a binding spell, and will only open to the correct password. If I still had my Crystal Lenses and my wand, I might be able to break the spell and open it. But I don't, so I can't." His lip trembles.

"Then we'd better start guessing magic words. Those rats are getting closer."

The three of you try every magic word you know. The old classics like "Open Sesame" and "Abracadabra" and "Hocus Pocus" and "Alakazam," then some of your favorite Ancient Elvish Words of Power. Zim tries lots of wizardly words, although to be honest, you suspect he's making some of them up. Nothing works.

A swarm of rats bursts from the far end of the cavern. Yeah, giant rats. Fast runners too.

"Got it!" Tina walks up to the carved face and says, "Please."

The face's mouth opens wide, revealing a small brightly lit room.

Tina grins. "Wow, Mom was right. 'Please' really is the magic word."

The three of you walk through the open mouth, and it snaps shut behind you.

"Great, we're safe from the giant rats, unless they're very polite talking giant rats," Zim says. "But now we're trapped again."

Or so it seems, until you notice *Level Exit* carved on the back of the mouth door.

You reach out and touch it, and suddenly you're back in the real world, soaking wet, sitting around the kitchen table with Jim and Tina. *Bonus Level Completed* is in big sparkly letters on your laptop screen.

"We won!" Tina says.

Jim snorts. "Won? I nearly drowned! My clothes are sopping wet, and I stink. Mom's going to yell at me."

"Remember to say 'please' and 'thank you' to her," you remind him as he squelches out.

"Not funny!"

"I'm serious. You too, Tina – your mom saved us."

"Yeah, sort of, maybe, I suppose. I'd better get home and out of these wet clothes. Back here next Saturday to play Level 101?"

Congratulations, you've finished this part of your story. Then again, if you'd made different choices, things might have gone even better (or much worse).

Have you met the Emerald Sage? Gotten lost in the

maze? Been attacked by the bone army? Said hello to the Reverse Dragon? Avoided the Zenobian Snapper?

It's time to make a decision. Do you:

Go back to the beginning of the story and try another path? **P113**

Or

Go to the great big list of choices? **P118**

Don't Help Zim

Sure, Zim's your friend, but not good enough a friend that you'd risk drowning.

He grabs at Tina, and she loses her balance too. Both of them fall into the bathtub water and sink without trace.

"Tina? Zim?"

Nothing. They're gone.

"Two down, one to go!" yells a watery voice from the tub.

The water spirits' splashes now get three times as bad, as they're aimed at you alone. Every time you take a step towards the hole you came through, the splashing gets worse, and you're nearly washed into the tub twice.

You look around, and spot another hole higher up the bathroom wall. Surely the water spirits can't splash that high? It's worth a try. Better than staying here, anyway.

So you start climbing, as fast as you can, holding on for dear life when the splashing gets too bad. As you climb out of range, they stop splashing and start yelling and cursing at you instead. Ignoring them, you concentrate on the hole above you, one handhold and one step at a time.

"Good riddance, two-legs, say hello to eight-legs!" is their final insult, as you clamber into the hole.

What did that mean?

Inside the hole, eyes stare at you, then long hairy legs grab you. Eight legs. Just as you finally realize (far too late) that it's a giant spider, it bites your arm. Everything turns black, and…

Suddenly you're back in the real world, sitting alone at the kitchen table, with a really sore arm. The words *Game Over* sparkle on your laptop screen. Huh?

Weren't you playing a computer game with someone, maybe two someones? Something about a giant bathtub? No, that doesn't make sense. Maybe you just imagined the whole thing.

Behind the table, a spider abseils down the wall, and you shiver.

Sorry, this part of your story is over. If you'd made different choices, things might have gone better (or even worse). Have you met the Emerald Sage? Gotten lost in the maze? Been attacked by the bone army? Said hello to the Reverse Dragon? Avoided the Zenobian Snapper?

It's time to make a decision. Do you:

Go back to the previous section? **P76**

Or

Go back to the beginning of the story and try another path? **P113**

Or

Go to the great big list of choices? **P118**

Sorry, Your Majesty

No, you'd rather not go through that hole – it could be a trap by Queen Moist.

"Sorry, your majesty, this is as far as we can take you," you tell her, very politely. She seems the sort to have a bad temper, and who knows what an angry water spirit might do.

"Obey me this instant, my minions!" she shrieks.

Your wet boots grow icicles. So do Zim's and Tina's boots.

"Quick, boots off before she freezes our feet solid!" shouts Tina.

You frantically fumble with your boots but can't unbuckle them.

"Impudent two-legs," the queen squeals. "Obey me while you can still walk!" She turns your wet boots scalding hot.

You're close to screaming in pain when suddenly your boots vanish. Tina and Zim are barefoot too. Through the hole comes splashing and yelling.

"What happened?" you ask.

Zim grins. "My super wizardly magic."

"I thought you couldn't fight elemental magic."

His grin gets wider. "I can't. That was the cleverest part – the queen was dragging us by the water in our boots, so I just cast Instantaneous Disintegration on the boots, and whoosh, she went with them before she realized my cunning plan."

Tina nods. "Thanks, Zim, smart move. Although now

we've got no boots."

"Moan, moan, moan. Anyone like a healing potion for their frozen blistered feet?"

He must be in a good mood – usually he won't hand out his precious potions unless someone gets an arm chopped off or worse.

The three of you sit and rub purple fizzy healing potion on your poor feet. Feels great.

Through the hole comes lots of shouting, mostly Queen Moist yelling orders, and lots of other voices yelling rude watery insults back.

"She doesn't sound like a very popular queen," Tina says. "Did you believe her 'all the gold you can carry' promise?"

"Nah," you say. "Had to be a scam. Let's get out of here. Unless you can cast us an Instant New Boots spell first, Zim?"

He sniffs. "Don't be silly, there's no such thing. I'm a wizard, not a shoe shop. Anyway, I've got a feeling that we're close to an exit."

So you all walk barefoot along the corridor and back past the wall of screaming skulls, trying to avoid the pointy gravel and spiders and rat poo on the floor.

Unfortunately, you're too busy avoiding stepping on yucky things, and so are totally surprised when a trapdoor opens beneath you.

You fall into a very deep dark hole, so deep that you keep falling, and falling, and falling. So deep that there's time for a long argument, all three of you blaming each other for not spotting the trapdoor. So deep that Zim has time to try casting various spells, none of which help in the slightest.

You point down. "I see the bottom. There's something there."

"Unless it's an enormous pile of soft cushions, I don't think it's going to help us," Tina says.

"Stop distracting me," Zim grumbles. He waves his wand again and turns into a giant chicken, but only for a few seconds. "Nearly had it that time!"

You look down, trying to work out what's below. Oh. It looks like a floor. A hard stone floor. The last thing you ever see is a ring of happy goblins looking up. The last thing you ever hear is "Here comes lunch!"

Sorry, this part of your story is over. If you'd made different choices, things might have gone better (or even worse). What would have happened if you'd helped the queen through the hole? Have you met the Emerald Sage? Gotten lost in the maze? Been attacked by the bone army? Said hello to the Reverse Dragon? Avoided the Zenobian Snapper?

It's time to make a decision. Do you:

Would you like to:

Go back to the previous section? **P71**

Or

Go back to the beginning of the story and try another path? **P113**

Or

Go to the great big list of choices? **P118**

So Hot

The three of you turn right and stroll up a gently sloping corridor for several minutes. It's deserted, and the only sign of danger is when you pass a small glowing blue pile on the floor – a goblin corpse, being nibbled by a swarm of slumberworms.

"Yuck," Zim says, and accidentally hits his head on the ceiling for the fifth time. "Ow."

"You should wear a steel helmet like me. Doesn't hurt at all." With a grin, Tina head-butts the ceiling.

The clang echoes up and down the corridor. The distant golden glow dims and flickers for a few seconds.

Her smile fades. "What was that?"

"A coincidence?" Zim whispers.

"Then why are you whispering?"

"In case it's not a coincidence."

The flickering has stopped. Whatever it was.

"Let's carry on," you say. "But be careful. The dwarves wouldn't have abandoned these tunnels without good reason. We're playing *Dungeon of Doom*, not *Ultra-Peaceful Happy Underground Walk of Absolutely No Danger*. Lots of nasty things are down here."

"What if it's something really, really dangerous?"

"Then it's probably the end-of-level monster guarding the exit. Isn't that what we're looking for?"

"Oh, yeah, I forgot."

You pass another glowing blue corpse. This one's a

spider, bigger than your head, covered in wiggling slumberworms.

Around a corner, the corridor slopes downwards towards an open doorway, the source of the mysterious golden glow. An equally mysterious rumble comes from the same doorway, as does a breeze of warm air and an odd smell.

"Maybe it's a fire demon," Tina says.

"Or central heating?" Zim suggests with a weak smile.

"Or a volcano," you say. "Hardly any slumberworms along here. Not sure whether that's good or bad."

You pass a side corridor blocked with rubble, then a couple of short charred skeletons. One's holding a dwarven axe and a fire-blackened gold necklace.

"This must be a trap," Zim says, looking around nervously. "I told you we should have gone the other way, down that nice damp cold corridor."

Tina snorts. "Yeah, yeah, maybe. After I get a good look through that doorway."

"Nice and slowly," you say. "In case we have to run."

Together, weapons drawn, you peer through the doorway. Inside is a steep narrow stone staircase with no handrail, leading downwards. From far above, beams of sunlight illuminate a room the size of a tennis court. The floor's heaped with gold and silver and jewels – the biggest treasure hoard you've ever seen, and the source of the golden glow.

Tina gasps, her eyes wide. "Wow. I mean...wow!" She starts down the staircase.

"Wait!" you say. "Like Zim said, this might be a trap. I

mean, who's going to leave a mountain of treasure lying around? Certainly not dwarves."

Zim frowns. "My Enchanted Shadow Crystal Lenses don't detect any magical traps. Do your elfy super-duper trap-detecting senses?"

"I haven't spotted any traps, no, but…come on, guys, there has to be something or someone guarding all that gold. And this room has no other exits, unless you can grow wings and fly up through that big hole in the ceiling. It's too dangerous."

"I'm ready for anything." Tina draws her sword and carries on down the stairs.

Zim looks longingly down at the treasure. "Sorry, Velzon, but…you know that old TV cartoon where the billionaire duck had a swimming pool full of money? I always thought that was so cool, and this is the closest I'll ever get." He follows Tina.

It's time to make a decision. Do you:

Follow them down the stairs? **P92**

Or

Leave them and escape? **P98**

Down the Stairs

For a moment, you're tempted to stay up here and let them be eaten or exploded or squashed or turned into purple bunny rabbits or whatever horrible fate must be waiting below.

But…you can't, coz they're your friends. They need you. And, to be really honest, swimming in money does sound like fun. So you follow them down the stairs.

Partway down, you realize the mysterious rumbling has stopped. Whatever it was.

"Look, I'm making a money angel," Zim says, lying on his back amongst the coins and waving his arms and legs back and forth.

"A what?" You're only half paying attention, still looking around for danger and still not spotting anything.

"A money angel – like a snow angel, but in money!"

"Oh, right."

"Wish I had my phone to take a selfie," Tina says, playing money angel too.

Giggling, she and Zim throw handfuls of diamonds at each other, causing a small avalanche in a nearby hill of treasure.

"So nice to see visitors enjoying themselves," says the deepest voice ever. The hill disintegrates as a huge dragon rises from underneath.

Oh, of course. Far too late, you notice bones scattered amongst the treasure.

"I so rarely get visitors, and when I do, they usually run away when they see me," the dragon continues, sounding offended.

It must be one of those talkative dragons. Good – maybe you can talk your way out of this. And it's not a fire breather – there's no gust of scorched air when it speaks – that's good too. Unless it just likes chatting with people before eating them.

"It's a great honor to meet you, your magnificence," you say, hoping your voice isn't shaking.

Tina and Zim take the hint.

"You're even more gloriously terrifying than I'd imagined," Tina says, bowing.

Zim bows too and takes off his hat. "Yeah, you're totally awesomely…um…awesome. Your majesty. Sir. Or ma'am." His knees are shaking.

The dragon smiles. "Such lovely manners. You're very kind, little wizard, but I'm not royalty. I do have eighty-seven crowns, though. Would you like one each as souvenirs?"

A dragon giving treasure away? You've never heard of that before. No, actually, there was something you read online last year, what was it again…

The dragon lashes out at Tina, so fast she doesn't have time to duck. But instead of killing her, it just knocks her helmet off.

"Erk," she says in a small voice.

The dragon gives her a spikey golden crown, shaped like

an angry skull with giant rubies for eyes. "This was the favorite battle crown of the mighty warlord Quoznar the Undying. Until he died."

"Cool!" She admires her reflection in a nearby silver tray. "Thanks heaps."

"It suits you, my dear," the dragon says. "Now, something suitable for a wizard and an elf, hmm, yes, perfect, where did I leave them?" It turns away, revealing an alarmingly large butt, and sifts through a hill of glittering jewelry.

Suddenly, you realize what's happening, and run over to Tina and Zim, holding a finger to your lips. "That's a Reverse Dragon. Zim, remember the Bright Shadow spell you used in Level 87?" you whisper, hoping the dragon doesn't overhear.

"What's a Reverse Dragon?"

"No time to explain! Cast Bright Shadow on us all, right now. It's our only chance."

He frowns and shrugs, then recites several lines of ancient Cobolese while waving his wand in weird spirals. Suddenly another Velzon, Zim and Tina stand next to you, or at least three fairly good imitations.

The dragon wiggles its butt. "Perhaps you could stay for lunch?"

"Thank you, your magnificence," you say, then race for the stairs, risking a quick glance back to confirm that Zim and Tina are following – the real Zim and Tina, that is.

The three fake yous, magical Bright Shadow mirages, stay

where they are. The dragon wiggles its butt again and farts orange flame over them. "Barbequed adventurers for lunch. My favorite," it roars happily.

You run up the stairs, not stopping, not even when something below clangs and Tina yells.

By the top of the stairs, you're out of breath, and so exhausted that you fall to the corridor floor when something pushes you from behind. Oh, it's Tina and Zim, both gasping for breath too.

"I dropped my beautiful scary battle crown," Tina wails.

"Good. It looked like a skull dipped in glitter," Zim mutters.

"Forget the stupid crown – where's the dragon?" You peer over the stairway, hoping to stay out of sight.

No such luck. The dragon's climbing the wall with long sharp claws. It spots you and speeds up. "Come back, my tasty, tricksy little snacks."

"Farty McFlameButt can't possibly squeeze through this little doorway," Tina says. "We're safe. Aren't we?"

"We're not out of fiery fart range yet."

Wearily, you all jog up the corridor slope. You pass the charred dwarf skeletons and fire-blackened gold necklace again. The dragon's previous victims? So, still not out of range.

"I can see you." The dragon's voice echoes up the corridor.

Glancing back, you see it maneuvering its butt to point through the doorway.

In desperation, you drag Zim and Tina into the short blocked side corridor. It's only a few yards deep, but it's the best – and only – cover available. "Maybe we can use the rubble to shield ourselves."

The three of you start heaving rocks and stones towards the main corridor, then drop to the ground as a jet of orange flame shoots past. It doesn't hit you, but Zim's tall wizard hat bursts into flame.

He squeals, pulls the hat off and bashes it against the wall, trying to extinguish the flames. Then stops, looks up and frowns. "Um, guys? Look."

Level Exit is carved on a stone ceiling slab.

He pulls out his wand and casts a Jackrabbit Jump spell. You all leap up and through the exit, just in time to avoid another jet of orange flame.

Suddenly you're back in the real world, sitting around the kitchen table with Jim and Tina, staring at *Bonus Level Completed* in big sparkly letters on your laptop screen.

"Did we win?" asks Tim.

"We survived," you say.

"My wizard hat was ruined," he grumbles.

"I lost my steel helmet," Tina mutters. "And that cool crown."

"We survived," you repeat.

She shrugs. "Anyone for Level 101?"

Congratulations, you've finished this part of your story. Then again, if you'd made different choices, things might have gone even better (or much worse). Have you met the Emerald Sage? Gotten lost in the maze? Been attacked by the bone army? Helped the extremely wet queen? Avoided the Zenobian Snapper?

It's time to make a decision. Do you:

Go back to the beginning of the story and try another path? **P113**

Or

Go to the great big list of choices? **P118**

Leave Them and Escape

No way are you following Zim and Tina down there. If those two fools want to die over some gold, that's their problem.

You head back up the corridor.

The sound of voices stops you. Tina, Zim, and an incredibly deep voice. You turn and look back at the glowing doorway.

If they're having a nice chat, then whoever it is can't be dangerous, right?

More talking, and the deep voice laughs. Not a nice laugh. Then there's screaming, horrible screaming, that stops suddenly, which is somehow even more horrible. A puff of warm air reaches you, smelling like a barbeque gone wrong.

Part of you wants to run away as fast as you can. Another part wants to go back and find out what happened. Yet another part of you has already guessed the worst.

Something passes the glowing doorway, then something else blocks it. Huh? Looks like…a huge scaly dragon butt? That makes no sense. The last thing you ever see is the butt farting a long jet of orange flame up the corridor, heading straight for you.

Sorry, this part of your story is over. If you'd made different choices, things might have gone better (or even worse). What would have happened if you'd followed Zim and Tina?

Have you met the Emerald Sage? Gotten lost in the maze? Been attacked by the bone army? Helped the extremely wet queen? Avoided the Zenobian Snapper?

It's time to make a decision. Do you:

Would you like to:

Go back to the previous section? **P89**

Or

Go back to the beginning of the story and try another path? **P113**

Or

Go to the great big list of choices? **P118**

Keep Running

No, absolutely anything could be in that dark room. Far too risky.

So you race past the doorway, around a corner, then screech to a stop in front of a gate of thick wrought iron bars.

The bars are bent, and the gate's been torn off one of its hinges. Behind the gate is a short corridor, ending in two doors facing each other.

The three of you squeeze through the gap around the broken hinge, then run up the corridor, past a dented "Do Not Feed the Animals" sign on the floor.

"What animals?" Tina asks.

"Maybe they escaped," you say. "I hope so. I don't want to meet whatever was strong enough to break that gate."

"Judging by the stinky smell, something's still here," Zim says.

The giant head thuds into the gate behind you, and pokes its long purple tongue through the bars. Clearly disappointed it can't reach anyone, it repeatedly rams the gate, which creaks and starts to bend.

"I reckon we've got maybe a minute before Big Head smashes through and licks us to death," Tina says. "What's through those doors?"

Both are solid oak, barred with stout ironwood beams, and have barred windows. These are serious doors, for keeping dangerous things in. Hmm, they'd also be good for keeping giant heads out.

Whatever's inside the left door is clucking like a deep-voiced chicken with a head cold, but is almost certainly far nastier.

You cautiously peer through the door's window and jump back as a barbed talon stabs at you and misses by an inch. "That's a Zenobian Snapper. Seven legs, all with talons like that. Super-fast and super-aggressive. Oh, and the talons are poisonous."

Zim and Tina frown.

Even more cautiously, you peer through the right door's window.

Nothing.

No, there in the shadows, a row of unblinking black eyes, silently watching, waiting.

"It's a Nammering," you continue. "Completely harmless at a distance. It waits until a victim gets too close, then grabs them and bites their head off. And it has four mouths – enough to bite all our heads off and still have a spare mouth to laugh at us at the same time."

Tina sighs. "Not much of a choice, is it?"

"I just had a crazy idea," Zim says. "What if I cast an Invisibility spell on us, then we open both doors at once, and let the Zenobian Snapper run over and attack the Nammering?"

Tina sighs again. "You're right, that is a crazy idea."

Or is it?

Behind you, the giant head rams the gate again.

It's time to make a decision, and fast. Do you:

Open both doors and hope the monsters fight each other? **P108**

Or

Open the left door and fight the Zenobian Snapper? **P103**

Or

Open the right door and fight the Nammering? **P105**

The Zenobian Snapper

You turn to the left door. "Zim, what magic do you have to help against a Zenobian Snapper?"

He pulls a tiny glass flask from a pocket inside his robe. "Negastic Sleeping Powder. Won't actually put a Snapper to sleep, but should slow it down. Then I can throw a few imploding fireballs."

Tina draws her sword. "And I can smite it lots. That'll help too."

"Well, yeah, I should hope so," you say, trying not to sound sarcastic. "I'll, um, shoot it with an arrow."

"Ooh, scary," Tina says, sounding extremely sarcastic. But you can tell she's just as scared as you are.

So's Zim. His hands shaking, he throws the flask through the door's window. It smashes on the floor inside. The weird clucking slows and stops. So far, so good.

Behind you, the giant head rams the gate yet again, and another hinge squeals and breaks. There's no time to lose.

Together, you lift the ironwood beam barring the door. Zim summons two silvery fireballs. You open the door, hoping to see a Zenobian Snapper yawning on the floor.

But the floor's empty, other than Zim's broken flask and a scattering of glittery powder.

Suddenly, a very awake Snapper drops from the ceiling, clucking happily. Before you have time to even scream, long talons lash out and stab you. The last thing you ever see is the inside of its jaws.

Sorry, this part of your story is over. If you'd made different choices, things might have gone better (or even worse). Have you met the Emerald Sage? Gotten lost in the maze? Been attacked by the bone army? Helped the extremely wet queen? Said hello to the Reverse Dragon?

It's time to make a decision. Do you:

Go back to the previous section? **P100**

Or

Go back to the beginning of the story and try another path? **P113**

Or

Go to the great big list of choices? **P118**

The Nammering

You turn to the right door. "Anyone fought a Nammering before?"

"Yeah, a few months ago," Tina says. "Well, I think so. Can't be one hundred percent sure. Whatever it was, it grabbed me and bit my head off before I had time to ask it any questions."

Zim rolls his eyes. "Thanks, that's so helpful."

"Are you a Nammering expert?"

"Well, I do know Nammerings like to hide in the dark, and they have great night vision. So how about a Sun Flash spell to dazzle it while we run past?" He rummages in his Big Book of Spells.

Behind you, the giant head rams the gate yet again. Another hinge squeals and breaks. There's no time to lose.

"Faster," you tell Zim.

"Okay, found it. Ready when you are." He raises his wand.

You and Tina lift the ironwood beam barring the door, then push the door open and stand back.

"Cover your eyes!" Zim warns.

Something flashes so brightly that you see a silhouette of the bones in your hand.

You lower your hand and open your eyes. The room looks empty.

Has the Nammering been frightened away?

Keeping her distance from any shadows, Tina leads the

way into the room. She stops mid-step. "Um, I just thought of an itsy-bitsy flaw in our plan. There can't be an exit in this room, coz if there was, the Nammering would have escaped through it long ago. So how exactly are we going to get out?"

Oh. Hadn't thought of that.

From outside comes the sort of noise you imagine a giant head would make when finally smashing through a wrought iron gate.

"Can we barricade the door?" you ask, pushing it closed.

It's a real fancy door – its inside is covered in elaborate carvings of strange animals. Why would someone go to the trouble of carving all over a door, and then use the room to keep a monster in?

Although maybe this room was never designed to hold monsters.

Too late, you notice the door's looking back at you with a row of black eyes. That's no carving, it's the Nammering lying in wait.

The last thing you ever see is it lunging at you, mouths wide open.

Sorry, this part of your story is over. If you'd made different choices, things might have gone better (or even worse).

Have you met the Emerald Sage? Gotten lost in the maze? Been attacked by the bone army? Helped the extremely wet queen? Said hello to the Reverse Dragon?

It's time to make a decision. Do you:

Go back to the previous section? **P100**

Or

Go back to the beginning of the story and try another path? **P113**

Or

Go to the great big list of choices? **P118**

Open Both Doors

"Let's try Zim's crazy idea," you say. "Like they say in eighties action movies, it's a million-to-one chance, but it just might work."

Zim grins, and Tina sighs.

Behind you, the giant head rams the gate yet again, and another hinge squeals and snaps. There's no time to lose. As risky as this plan is, you have to do it right now.

Zim flicks through his Big Book of Spells and hurriedly casts an Invisibility spell on all three of you.

Together, you lift the ironwood beams barring the doors.

Tina opens the Nammering's door. There's no reaction from inside.

You open the Snapper's door, hoping you're completely and totally invisible – otherwise the Zenobian Snapper might decide to kill you instead of the Nammering.

The plan works perfectly. Ignoring you, the Snapper charges into the other room and attacks the Nammering. You can't see who's winning, and judging by the horrible noises they're making, you don't want to see.

Seconds later, the giant head smashes through the gate, and races into the same room to join the "fun". Even better.

You close and bar the Nammering's door, just in case. Zim dispels the Invisibility spell. High fives all around.

"You're not as crazy as you look, Zim," Tina says.

"Thanks." He smiles.

That's the nicest thing she's said to him in weeks.

"Hmm, there can't be an exit in the Snapper's room – if there was, the Snapper would have used it ages ago." You look back down the corridor and the gate wreckage. "So I guess we'll have to go back the way we came. At least we don't have to worry about the giant head any more."

Something in the Nammering's room roars, as if agreeing.

"Let's at least have a look in the Snapper's room. There could be treasure or something." Tina goes in, not waiting for you and Zim.

"Or hundreds of baby Snappers," Zim grumbles, but follows her anyway.

The room stinks. The stone floor is littered with well-gnawed bones, some of them fresh, and dented armor and broken weapons. No baby monsters, though.

Zim toes some glittery powder by a tiny broken glass flask. "Looks like Negastic Sleeping Powder. Someone thought they could put a Zenobian Snapper to sleep. Very risky."

Tina's more interested in a small alcove. "Hey, guys, maybe there is an exit after all."

It doesn't look like much, just a round narrow tunnel sloping gently downwards. Far too small for the Snapper, but you three could squeeze through on your hands and knees. A gentle breeze of fresh air blows out of it – well, fresher than the other air in here.

Zim frowns. "Crawling through an air vent? Like in one of Velzon's eighties action movies?"

"Why not? Even Zenobian Snappers need to breathe."

You climb into the tunnel and start crawling. Tina and Zim follow.

A few yards in, the whole tunnel suddenly tilts. You tumble down a steep slope and fall onto a stone floor. Tina falls on you. Zim falls on Tina. Ouch.

It's a generic stone-walled dungeon corridor, lit by burning torches. Seems familiar somehow. Very familiar. After listening and sniffing in both directions, you sigh. "This is the same corridor we started from. Goblins to the left. Ogres to the right."

Tina swears under her breath and kicks the wall. "Left. We went right last time, and look how that turned out."

"No, we should go right again," Zim insists. "It'll be easy this time – we've already cleared out most of the monsters."

They look at you. It's time to make a decision. Do you:

Go left, towards the goblins? **P7**

Or

Go right, towards the ogres? **P111**

Ogres Again

You turn right and advance down the corridor.

Just like last time, the ogres run past, followed by a giant rolling head. Just like last time, you run.

"Is that the same giant head or a different one?" Zim asks, puffing as he follows you.

"Who cares?" Tina says. "Where's that dark open doorway we didn't try last time? Has it disappeared?"

"There it is!" You run through it, and smash into a wall. "Ow!"

Tina and Zim thud into your back.

"Double ow!"

The ceiling suddenly glows, showing that the room's only a few feet deep and wide.

"This is a dead end!" Tina snarls. "I told you we should have turned left!"

Outside, the giant head rolls to a stop. It can't fit through the doorway, any more than the other giant head could fit through the wrought iron gate, but its long purple tongue grabs your leg and pulls.

The room's metal door starts to slide closed by itself, hits the tongue, and stops.

"Stab it!" Tina shouts.

You draw your dagger.

"No, tickle it! Trust me, Velzon!" Zim shouts.

It's time to make a decision. Do you:
Stab the tongue? **P66**
Or
Tickle the tongue? **P68**

Back at the Beginning

On Saturday morning, you're sitting around the kitchen table with Jim and Tina, playing *Dungeon of Doom* together on your laptops.

"Gotcha." Jim taps his keyboard to launch another fireball at the Nine-Headed Dragon's eleventh head. (One head grew back. Twice.)

"Yee ha!" Tina's onscreen avatar, Tina Warrior Princess, finally chops off the dragon's last head.

Level Completed appears in giant sparkly letters. The floor of the dungeon room fills with end-of-level bonuses. Your avatar, Velzon the Elven Archer, runs around the room collecting them. Tina Warrior Princess and Jim's avatar, Wizard Zim, do the same.

"Warriors don't say 'yee ha'," Jim complains.

Okay, you know what happens next – you see the weird shimmering circle on the wall, and finally the others stop bantering and see it too.

Onscreen, you pick up a gold coin and toss it at the shimmery wall. As you'd half-expected, the coin vanishes. At the same moment, the edge of the circle flashes like a camera, spelling out words.

"It says 'Secret Bonus Level' in Klodruchian runes," you say.

Cool.

Onscreen, Tina Warrior Princess and Velzon and Zim leap into the shimmering portal at the same time. Everything turns really bright, then really dark, then…

Huh? The kitchen's gone, and you're lying on a stone floor. Next to you are a tall woman covered in muscles and scars and battered armor, and a bearded guy in a purple robe and a pointy hat – Tina Warrior Princess and Wizard Zim, looking just like they do in the game, but…now they're real.

Impossible. Totally impossible.

"What happened?" Wizard Zim asks.

You look down. You're wearing Velzon's leaf-embroidered jerkin, spider silk trousers, and lizard-leather boots. Just to be sure, you reach up, and…yup, elf ears. On your back is a bow and quiver. On your belt is a long dagger of finest Kargalin steel. Exactly like in the game.

"We're inside *Dungeon of Doom*." Tina Warrior Princess stands up, a huge grin on her scarred face. "Cool!"

Zim tugs at his beard. "Don't be stupid. We can't be. What is this, some new virtual reality thing?" He turns to you. "I don't like it. Make it stop. Turn it off. Now!"

"How?" you ask.

He runs around the room, yelling, "Reset! End game! Escape! Power off! End simulation! Exit!" Nothing happens.

"Let's explore!" Tina shouts, and runs out the room's only doorway.

"We might as well. We can't just stay here," you tell Zim.

"Mmm," he says reluctantly, and follows you through the doorway.

Tina's only a few steps away, frowning as she looks up

and down a corridor. "This better not be a maze. I hate mazes. Always get lost." She says it like she's joking, but it's the truth – she has a terrible sense of direction, in real life and in games.

Left and right look the same – generic stone-walled dungeon corridors, lit by burning torches, with more doorways in the distance. This level's exit could be either way. Or both ways – some levels have more than one exit.

Zim peers both ways through his Enchanted Shadow Crystal Lenses, then shrugs and looks at you. "Well, pointy ears?"

After listening and sniffing in both directions, you point left. "Goblins. Lots of them." You point right. "Ogres. Coming this way."

Tina and Zim look at you expectantly.

"What, you want *me* to decide?"

Tina grins. "Yeah, Velzon, you're good at that elfy scouting stuff. That's the only reason we let you play with us."

Zim nods. "Let's play this level the same way we usually do – you leading the way."

"So I get shot first, and stabbed first, and zapped first?" you ask.

"No worries, we'll be right behind, ready to rescue you," Tina says.

"And I've got a zillion healing potions if you get injured," Zim says.

"Thanks, you two are so helpful."

It's time to make a decision. Do you:

Go left, towards the goblins? **P7**

Or

Go right, towards the ogres? **P63**

More You Say Which Way Adventures

Deadline Delivery
Between The Stars
Pirate Island
Lost in Lion Country
Once Upon An Island
In the Magician's House
Secrets of Glass Mountain
Danger on Dolphin Island
Volcano of Fire
Deadline Delivery
The Creepy House
Stranded Starship
Dragons Realm
Dinosaur Canyon
Mystic portal

Or try a You Say Which Way Adventure Quiz

The Sorcerer's Maze Adventure Quiz
The Sorcerer's Maze Jungle Trek
The Sorcerer's Maze Time Machine

List of Choices

Secret Bonus Level...1

The Goblins 7

Invisibly Sneak Past the Goblins............................10

Chop the Ivy..14

Follow the Ivy...16

Run for It...21

Break the Spell..23

The Narrow Doorway..32

The White Door..36

Don't Open the Purple Door..................................39

The White Door..41

The Yellow Door...42

Throw the egg to the Dwarves...............................49

Throw the egg to the Shark...................................51

The Purple Door..53

The Yellow Door...58

The Purple Door..59

Ogres, Rock and Roll...63

Dark Room...65

Stabby Stabby..66

Tickly Tickly..68

So Cool...71

Swimming Pool (or is it?) 76

Help Zim..79

Don't Help Zim 84

Sorry, Your Majesty 86

So Hot..89

Down the Stairs...92

Leave Them and Escape 98

Keep Running..100

The Zenobian Snapper..103

The Nammering 105

Open Both Doors 108

Ogres Again 111

Back at the Beginning...113

More You Say Which Way Adventures.............117

Or try a You Say Which Way Adventure Quiz 117

List of Choices...118

Preview: Deadline Delivery...................................121

Please leave a review of this book on Amazon 125

About Peter Friend 127

Preview: Deadline Delivery

Out of breath from climbing stairs, you finally reach Level 8 of Ivory Tower. Down the hallway, past a tattoo parlor, Deadline Delivery's neon sign glows red. The word Dead flickers as you approach.

It's two minutes past seven in the morning – is Deadline Delivery's dispatch office open yet? Yes, through the mesh-covered window in the steel door, Miss Betty is slouched behind her cluttered desk. You knock and smile as if you want to be here.

Miss Betty turns and scowls at you. Nothing personal – she scowls at everyone. She presses a button and the steel door squeaks and squeals open.

"Good morning, ma'am. Got any work for me today?" you ask.

She sighs, scratches her left armpit, and taps at her computer. Then she rummages through a long shelf of packages and hands you a plastic-wrapped box and two grimy dollar coins. "Urgent delivery," she says. "Pays ten bucks, plus toll fees."

Ten dollars is more than usual. Suspicious, you check the box's delivery label. "390 Brine Street? That's in the middle of pirate territory!"

She shrugs. "If you're too scared, there are plenty of other kids who'll do it."

Scared? You're terrified. But you both know she's right – if you don't take this job, someone else will. And you really need the money – you have exactly three dollars in the whole world, and your last meal was lunch yesterday. "Thank you, Miss Betty."

"Uniform," she says, pointing to the box of Deadline Delivery caps.

You pick up the least dirty cap. What's that stink? Has something died in it? You swap it for the second-least dirty one and put that on. You'd rather not wear any kind of uniform – sometimes it's better to not attract attention in public – but Miss Betty insists.

The steel door squeaks and starts to close, and you hurry out. Miss Betty doesn't say goodbye. She never does.

After stashing the package in your backpack and the toll coins in your pocket, you hurry down the stairs to the food court on Level 5. Time to grab a quick breakfast. This might be your last meal ever, and there's no sense in dying hungry. This early in the morning, only Deep-Fried Stuff and Mac's Greasy Spoon are open, so there's not a lot of choice.

In Mac's Greasy Spoon, Mac himself cuts you a nice thick slice of meatloaf for a dollar, and you smile and thank him, even though his meatloaf is always terrible.

If there's any meat in it, you don't want to know what kind. At least it's cheap and filling. After a few bites, you wrap the rest in a plastic bag and put it in your pocket for lunch.

You walk back down the stairs to Ivory Tower's main entrance on Level 3. Levels 1 and 2 are somewhere further down, underwater, but you've never seen them. The polar ice caps melted and flooded the city before you were born.

From beside the bulletproof glass doors, a bored-looking guard looks up. "It's been quiet out there so far this morning," she tells you, as she checks a security camera screen. "But there was pirate trouble a few blocks north of the Wall last night. And those wild dogs are roaming around again too. Be careful, kid."

The doors grind open, just a crack, enough for you to squeeze through and out onto Nori Road. Well, everyone calls it a road, although the actual road surface is twenty feet under the murky water.

Both sides of the so-called road have sidewalks of rusty girders and planks and bricks and other junk, bolted or welded or nailed to the buildings – none of it's too safe to walk on, but you know your way around.

Just below the worn steel plate at your feet, the water's calm. Everything looks quiet. No boats in sight. A few people are fishing out their windows. Fish for breakfast? Probably better than meatloaf.

Far over your head, a mag-lev train hums past on a rail bridge. Brine Street's only a few minutes away by train – for rich people living up in the over-city. Not you.

Mac once told you that most over-city people never leave the sunny upper levels, and some of them don't even don't know the city's streets are flooded down here. Or don't care, anyway. Maybe that's why there are so many security fences between up there and down here, so that over-city people can pretend that under-city people like you don't exist.

There are fences down here too. To your left, in the distance, is Big Pig's Wall – a heavy steel mesh fence, decorated with spikes and barbed wire and the occasional skeleton. The same Wall surrounds you in every direction, blocking access above and below the waterline – and Brine Street's on the other side. The extra-dangerous side.

Big Pig's Wall wasn't built to keep people in – no, it's to keep pirates out.

The heavily guarded Tollgates are the only way in or out, and to go through them, everyone has to pay a toll to Big Pig's guards. A dollar per person, more for boats, all paid into big steel-bound boxes marked Donations. Big Pig has grown rich on those "donations". Not as rich as over-city people, but still richer than anyone else in this neighborhood. Some people grumble that Big Pig and his guards are really no better than the pirate gangs, but most locals think the tolls are a small price to pay for some peace and security.

Then again, you happen to know the Tollgates *aren't* the only way in and out – last week, you found a secret tunnel that leads through the Wall. No toll fees if you go that way – two dollars saved. You finger the coins in your pocket.

It's time to make a decision.

How will you get to Brine Street? Do you:

Go the longer and safer route through a Tollgate?

Or

Save time and money, and try the secret tunnel?

Please leave a review of this book on Amazon

Reviews help others know if this book is right for them.
It only takes a moment.
Thanks from the You Say Which Way team.

About Peter Friend

Peter Friend lives in New Zealand, where there are earthquakes, giant squid, and the world's largest insect – the weta. He looks a bit like a dwarf, although was unsuccessful getting a job as an extra in the *Lord of the Rings* and *Hobbit* movies. The only magical power he has is world building with words. And muffin baking.

This is his second interactive adventure book, after *Deadline Delivery* in 2015. Yes, *Dungeon of Doom* starts with D and D too. He seems to be a bit obsessed with D if you ask me. I mean, what's next - *Dangerous Delicatessen? The Dozen Dizzy Dalmatians? Dreadful Dastardly Dinosaur Denizens from Downstairs? The Delicious Double Dessert Diet?* Actually, that one sounds rather good. Now I'm feeling a bit peckish.

Peter Friend has written fiction, plays and articles for numerous magazines and anthologies around the world. He also makes short films. If you leave him a review, we might be able to convince him to write more You Say Which Ways.

YouSayWhichWay.com

Printed in Great Britain
by Amazon

68039509R00080